Auspicious Journey

THE GIFT OF
PEACE
IN A TIME OF WAR

BRUCE JUNIOR WEST

Hawkeye Publishers

For more information, please address Hawkeye Publishers
HawkeyePublishers.com

Library of Congress Control Number: 2018940922

Paperback: 978-1946005-199
Hardcover: 978-1946005-182
Ebook: 978-1946005-205

This book is dedicated to Ong De.

LAOS

Hanoi
•

NORTH
VIET
NAM

Hue
•
Hoa An • Da Nang
•

SOUTH
VIET
NAM

CAMBODIA

Saigon
•

Introduction

If you're looking for another war story, you may be disappointed. Since the time of Homer, military histories and stories of combat have been published with glowing accounts of duty, honor, and glory. This is not one of them.

This book documents the Vietnam war as it occurred to the men and women, as well as the children and elders of a village in Vietnam. If their stories were told as often as those of the warriors, we might think much harder and longer before going to war again and again.

The purpose of this book is to convey the struggle of a village trying to survive the war and what the people of that community taught me in the process.

Every veteran's experience is unique and personal. Each deserves to be honored and remembered in its own right. As a work of fiction, this novel includes a variety of characters and events. The names of these individuals and locations have been changed out of respect for their privacy and safety.

Like many veterans, I am proud of my service in Vietnam. It was the best work I have ever done in the most difficult of circumstances. I am often asked how I am able to remember these people and these events so vividly. I wonder how I can ever forget.

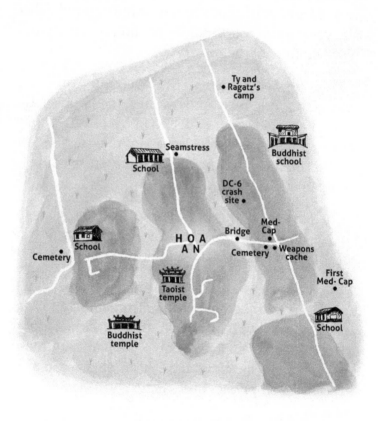

Village of Hoa An

Chapter 1

It was January 1968, in Quang Nam Province, Republic of South Vietnam. Dan was sitting in a truck watching the red ball of the morning sun rising through the smoke and ash of the bloody, ruined sky.

Trapped at a busy intersection by a vibrant throng of refugees, school children, farmers, and mothers on their way to market, he found himself fascinated by the ebb and flow of their strangely mater-of-fact existence. This place, on the other side of the planet, seemed so completely different from anything he had ever imagined. The cab of the truck was inundated by intense heat and crushing humidity. It felt like an oven, baking the strange sights, sounds and smells into every sweating pore of the person he used to be.

Dan understood that his truck was an easy target for a Viet Cong satchel charge. It could also be swarmed and stripped by gangs of black-market pirates. But there was nothing he could do but sit and sweat in the blast furnace heat of the sun flooding through the dirty windshield.

There were no sewers and water was drawn from a community well. Too many people had lived too close together for too long. The smells had joined with the extreme heat and humidity until there was no air fit to breathe.

An impossibly overloaded Pedi-cab, stuffed with stoic, uncomplaining Vietnamese beep–beeped its way along the blacktop pavement. The cab stopped and a schoolgirl in a clean, white Ao Dai (native formal dress) stepped out onto the shoulder with her books. Perfectly erect and spotlessly clean, she serenely navigated her way through the chaos. A young South Vietnamese soldier, his wife holding on to him with one arm and their baby with the other, carefully threaded their motorbike through the living tapestry of war-torn Quang Nam Province.

A South Vietnamese Army vehicle stalled and blocked traffic long enough for Dan to rev the International truck he was driving and move forward into the intersection. Turning left onto Highway One, he entered the human river flowing through the constantly shifting uncertainties of life in wartime.

The ancient port city of Da Nang sat on a beak of land pointing toward the South China Sea. On the north, it was bordered by the Bay of Da Nang, and on the east by the Da Nang River. Running north, Highway One passed west of the city, turning sharply to follow the long perfect arc of the bay up to the Truong Son mountains, the Hi Van Pass and on up to the ancient city of Hue.·

The village of Hoa An sat in the corner where the highway turned west. Hoa An was made up of four hamlets. A traveler entering the village would find two hamlets along the west side of the road, a broad open field of rice, and then two more hamlets farther west. A network of worn pathways connected the hamlets with their temples, schools and marketplaces. There were two graveyards, one on each side of the rice field.

The people built their homes and lived in the park-like shade of the bamboo forest. The two hamlets nearest the road were swollen with refugees, while the two farther away from the road seemed more able to maintain the traditional values of village life.

Beginning with the Moro Wars in the Philippines, the Marine Corps had developed a program of civic action to support the stability of local governments. Teams of especially motivated and trained Marines were placed in the local villages after the larger combat units had passed through. In addition to supporting the local communities, it served to prevent guerrilla forces from rising up and attacking the Marines from the rear. Proven successful in the Philippines, it was later adopted in Vietnam.

Sharing the same organizational structure as the Marines, the Seabees followed suit, except instead of a squad, or platoon of men, it was only Dan and his partner Steve.

For the most part, the young Seabees were a good team. They were both well educated and were curious about the Vietnamese. Steve was short, dark haired, lean and intense, with a special grace and maturity in his dealings with others. He was from the east coast, Dan from the west. Steve had been branded Catholic at an early age and was determined to always do the right thing. Dan, taller, with sun bleached hair, had grown up on the beaches of California, embraced the emerging counter-culture, and had no illusions about authority. Regardless of their differences, they recognized each other's strengths and worked well outside the normal chain of command.

They were assigned to support the officials of the local government of Hoa An any way they could. Given a truck and a badge they were permitted to enter the Vietnamese cities and villages that were off limits to other American service men. They decided that their first effort to introduce themselves would be by organizing a temporary medical clinic, or Med-Cap, in the village.

Leaving the crowded intersection, Dan drove the stake bed International about a mile and a half north to where a small concrete block building sat alone on the left-hand side of the road. Separated from the shanties by a stand of bamboo, it looked as if it might have once served as a provincial office. But now, behind its barred and vacant windows, it was dark, empty, and uninviting.

Carefully crossing through the thinning traffic, Dan pulled onto the wide shoulder, stopped and turned off the motor. The truck shuddered and died.

Peering through the dirty windshield Steve said, "This is where we're supposed to set up for the Med-Cap."

Dan looked at the empty building but didn't say anything.

The Doctor and Corpsmen had followed in a jeep. Watching in the rear-view mirror he saw them stop behind the truck. They didn't get out. The Doctor sat stiff in the seat. This was everyone's first time in the village, and nobody was too sure what to expect.

He asked Steve, "Why here?"

"This is where they said."

"Who said?"

"The Senior Chief."

He could tell Steve wasn't too thrilled about holding the Med-Cap at this location. Neither was he. Although the Senior Chief was the highest-ranking enlisted man in the Battalion he was not part of the normal chain of command, and they did not work for him. Dan wondered what the Senior Chief had to do with the decision to hold the Med-Cap here.

One of the Corpsmen, Bobby Burden, jumped out of the jeep and started setting up the supplies for the Med-Cap.

He grinned at Dan, "Let's get this thing goin'!"

Dan agreed. He'd been in the truck long enough. It felt good to get out and get his feet on the ground. At least here, in the village of Hoa An, the stench was not so bad.

Mouth to mouth, shanty to shanty, word traveled fast. Painfully thin refugees in worn, gray clothing emerged from the rows of shanties made of everything from sheets of cardboard to wooden pallets discarded by the military. Villagers and refugees hurried along the side of the road to stand in a quiet line that was getting longer every time he looked.

"What are we dealing with, Bobby?"

"You name it. As you can tell by the smell there's no sewers. They get their water from a central well. There's malaria, hepatitis, tuberculosis, and no medical service of any kind."

"Except us?"

Bobby nodded, "Except us."

Bobby waved north toward the blue shadow of the Truong Son Mountains running east into the

South China Sea. "There's even a leper colony up there."

Dan looked at the mountains in the far distance, his eye following the ridgeline down and east toward the sea. He tried to imagine the poor souls with leprosy. He wondered what their life was like squatting, gazing out at the sea, isolated forever from everyone and everything they had ever loved.

Bobby went on, "You got shots for all this at Hueneme, right?"

Dan nodded. He remembered shot day at Port Hueneme. He had walked slowly down the long hall of the medical wing, receiving shot after shot in both arms. Big strong guys were passing out from the shots. Other guys held them up against the walls, easing them down to the floor.

At the end of the hall, he followed the line of men through the open door to the porch outside and dropped his pants for the gamma globulin shot. It felt like being kicked hard in the rump, serving to launch him down the steps to the sidewalk where he pulled up his pants, deemed ready for war.

He got a shot for the black plague spread by the rats and the fleas they carried. He remembered getting the shots and how it had occurred to him that he was not just going to the other side of the planet, but also to what seemed like a distant time.

He remembered reading the story of Dr. Thomas Dooley, the Navy doctor who had treated thousands of Vietnamese refugees following the partitioning of the nation in 1954. Even as a child, Dan had been impressed by Dooley's commitment to helping those refugees who had fled from Hanoi to Da Nang. The overwhelming numbers of desperate people, the shortage of medical supplies, and the makeshift nature of the 'clinic' reminded Dan of the conditions described by Dooley.

Dan was intrigued by the possibility that some of the people treated today could be the descendants of those treated by Dr. Dooley.

He felt like he was in good company. Like the good Doctor, Dan clung to the belief that, in some small way, he might have an opportunity to mitigate the horrors of this war. Like the good Doctor, he hoped to somehow shine a tiny ray of hope in one person's heart, a slender marker on the wall of time.

Bobby caught his eye and grinned. "It's Medieval, Dan. The Middle Ages. The rats carry the fleas and the fleas carry the plague. We got lots of both."

Bobby stood, stretched, and went on. "The biggest problem is because of the war, there's no soap and no disinfectant. Even though they try to stay clean, an insect bite or a small scratch can get badly infected, even fatal, especially to an infant."

Bobby gestured to a woman in the line. She was holding a tiny baby. Barely breathing, it lay limp and motionless in her arms. Dan looked down at the medical supplies that seemed so small and clean and out of place.

Bobby looked at Dan and said, "Sometimes there's just not much we can do."

What had started as a group of curious villagers soon grew to a crowd of eighty or ninety refugees. The crowd was still growing. Dan could see an endless line of desperate souls silently hurrying toward them, skimming over the hard ground in their brown plastic sandals.

The villagers had a sense that the Corpsmen's supplies would not be enough to treat them all. When the first patient was chosen the crowd's silent reserve broke down, and they surged forward pleading to be seen.

Dan had just enough Vietnamese language school to be polite. However, everyone was now talking at once, trying to be heard, their urgent voices joining in a riot of strange sounds that overwhelmed his meager understanding of the language.

He felt a small hand slide into his front pocket and take his wallet. It was gone before he could do anything about it. Frantic, he looked around but had no idea who had taken it. It contained little more than his I.D. and his picture of Lilly. How could he explain to the Battalion that a child had stolen his I.D?

"Ouch!"

Someone reached through the crowd and pulled some hair out of his arm, then did it again. Wondering what would happen next, he saw the blond hairs from his arm passing from one set of curious hands to another. Chattering excitedly, they looked at the hairs, held them up to the sunlight, and passed them on. He saw the contents of his wallet circulating through the crowd in the same way. They seemed to be as curious about him as he was about them.

Just before the Corpsmen ran out of meds, Dan felt the same small hand slide the wallet back into his pants pocket. He looked quickly to see if he could catch the pickpocket in the act, but all he saw was a child's small, brown arm disappearing back into the crowd.

He circled the Med-Cap with his M16, unable to understand how to maintain any sense of order or safety in this world that defied everything he had ever known. Six-feet tall and blond from the sun of the California beaches, he stuck out over the chaos like an advertisement for American good intentions.

Chapter Two

Hoping the war in Vietnam would somehow pass them by, Dan and Lilly were married during the spring break of 1967. They moved into a little house in the hills above San Luis Obispo, where they lived rent-free in exchange for taking care of the property and its horses.

One evening they sat on a bench in front of the house. They watched the sun go down along a line of granite peaks that stretched down the valley and on into the ocean. Seeking his warmth, Lilly leaned into him as the darkness gently closed around them. Startled by her beauty and his desire for her, he held her close, sharing the heat from their bodies touching.

"Want to go in?" he asked.

She didn't say anything, just looked up at him, smiled and rested her head against his chest.

When they could bear it no longer, they went inside the little house to lay together in their second-hand bed, marveling at the urgent beauty of their young bodies and their great good fortune of being together. In the morning, they stayed in bed, relaxing in the warmth of the new day as the alligator lizards ran in and out through the cracks in the block wall.

They pruned and watered the seriously neglected rose bushes and watched them come into bloom while they waited, hoping to escape the deadly tentacles of a corrupt draft.

But they didn't. Dan's student deferment finally ran out. He had already been to Los Angeles for his physical and knew it would only be a few short weeks before he would be ordered to report to the Army.

Hoping to stay out of Vietnam, he joined the Navy. He had earned his way through school working construction, so he was not surprised when he was assigned to the Navy's combat engineers at Port Hueneme, "Homeport of the Pacific SeaBees."

He said good-by to Lilly and took the Greyhound down the coast. Sitting alone, he watched the big, blue Pacific, stretching away to Pearl and Guam and Subic Bay and the warm waters of the South China Sea.

The bus was almost empty. Dan sat behind a first class Petty Officer in a dated and worn Navy uniform. He told Dan that he had been in Korea and was now joining up for Vietnam. Dan told him he was reporting to the Seabees and would most likely end up in Vietnam.

The old warrior turned part way around and said, "Don't believe everything they tell you." Looking out the window he went on. "Everything changes when the shootin' starts."

Dan didn't know what to say, but somehow he wasn't surprised.

The old veteran continued. "Hook up with someone who's been there and listen to 'em.

"We like to think our military is the best in the world, but from what I've seen it was the Turks. They been fighting as long as they can remember, and it seems like they were born with a knife in their hands.

"All I can say it was a good thing they were on our side in Korea. I would be in my hole at night, so black I couldn't see my hand in front of my face, and then I'd feel their fingers on my neck. I'd never hear 'em comin' or goin'. I'd just be sitting there scared shitless and then they'd be reaching around my neck, feeling for my dog tags. And you better believe I made sure I had them right where they were supposed to be. Some guys got their throats cut 'cause they didn't."

Dan didn't say anything.

"The Koreans were better than we gave 'em credit for. Hell, armies been stompin' up and down that peninsula forever an' they just get tougher and tougher."

He paused, "There's some South Korean troops in Vietnam, huh?"

"I don't know," Said Dan. "I guess so."

As the bus pulled into the Oxnard station, the old warrior chuckled to himself and turned around. He looked at Dan across the back of the seat. "They'll tell you your weapon is your best friend. It ain't."

Dan was listening.

"That'd be your shovel. When the shootin' starts, dig in' and don't stop. Just keep on diggin'. Some guys said 'ta hell with it, that's deep enough,' and in the morning they'd be dead."

Dan asked him, "Where are you going now?"

"I don't know, wherever they take me, I guess."

"Good luck to you," Dan said shaking his hand.

"Same to you son. Same to you."

Dan watched the Petty Officer pick up his worn sea bag and drag it out of the bus to the next war.

He thought about the old sailor as the bus passed under the sign at Port Hueneme that said, "We Build -We Fight." Dan was surprised to see everyone dressed in Marine Corps greens. He thought he had joined the Navy. The "We Fight!" sign made him wonder what the old sailor on the bus would think.

Chapter Three

Dressed in Marine Corps greens like everyone else, Dan stepped out of the hard, soaking rain and walked down the long hallway that smelled of disinfectant and floor wax. All the walls, all the doors, everything was painted the exact same shade of Sea Foam Green. A Seabee was riding a buffer, polishing the same floor he had polished the day before and the day before that.

Dan went into the Headquarters Company Office, and asked the clerk if he had any orders.

"Yep, an' it's your lucky day." The clerk handed him the sheet of paper that would define the rest of his life.

He took it and looked at the big color map of Vietnam hanging on the wall. He'd been assigned to a unit so close to North Vietnam that he couldn't tell which side of the DMZ it was on.

He pointed at the map. "Look, I don't want to complain or anything, but you're sending me to North Vietnam." He meant it as a joke but no one seemed to get it, or maybe they got it and didn't think it was funny.

The clerk shrugged and said, "Yeah, well, who knows anything for sure? The last I heard, that Battalion was moving down toward Da Nang."

Dan ran to their little car through the driving rain and sat behind the wheel, looking at the orders he had tried so hard to avoid. He was going to Vietnam. Now that he knew, he had to tell Lilly.

Preparing for deployment to Vietnam, the Battalion had canceled all leaves, and everyone had been ordered to report from off base housing. What about Lilly? He wasn't ready to leave her. Still in denial that he would have to leave, they had not said their goodbyes. She was waiting for him in their empty apartment in Ventura. The Seabees would have him for a year. He decided to spend those last few days with her.

He had never planned on going AWOL (absent without leave) but there was no doubt in his mind that his first duty was to her. He filled the car with gas and left the base by the main gate. Stopping under the sign that said "We Build - We Fight", he waited for traffic to clear, looked both ways and turned onto the wet city streets of Port Hueneme. He knew it would be a problem when he didn't show up for muster that night, but it didn't matter. Like the guys said, "What were they going to do, send him to Vietnam?"

He drove up the coast to Ventura where Lilly was waiting for him. She was flying out of Los Angeles the next day, but for now they were broke with nowhere to spend the night. One of his friends in the Seabees had moved out of his apartment, and Dan had given him most of what little money he had left for a key to the place. He didn't tell Lilly he was AWOL and she didn't ask.

Dodging the raindrops, the two of them climbed the wet concrete steps to the second-floor apartment. With nowhere else to go, he hoped it would be adequate to somehow meet the needs of their last night together.

He pushed the door open and watched her face as she looked at the empty room with the mattress on the floor. He could tell they were not going to spend their last night together in this place.

He had been issued a Texaco gas card while in college. He had never used it, but one of the guys had mentioned that there was a new high-rise hotel in Encino that might accept it.

He threw the mattress in a dumpster behind the apartment building and they drove on to Los Angeles through the worst storm to hit Southern California in over a hundred years. The creeks and rivers were filled with brown water rushing down the steep mountainsides. South Ventura was flooded with water and debris battered the bottom of the 101 bridge. Their little car sputtered along, leaking badly through the convertible top, threatening to lose a cylinder, or quit all together.

The short, bleak day turned dark, then black. The wind and the rain buffeted the car as they drove on through the storm. Fighting for every mile, they finally checked into the nearly deserted hotel.

Dan pushed the card across the counter top and the clerk took it without question. They asked for a room on the top floor. Except for Lilly's luggage, everything they owned was in soggy brown paper grocery bags. The bellman graciously escorted them to their room, and Dan tipped him a dollar, which, except for their little car, was one quarter of their total net worth.

They spent the night together watching the lights of the cars in the rain on the freeway below. The stark reality that they might never see each other again hung in the silence between them. They were painfully aware that these last few moments could very well be the sum total of their life together.

The rain on the glass blurred the lights of the cars. He and Lilly stood at the window watching through the wet glass. Holding on to each other as the night slipped away, they shared a desperate, unspoken commitment to be together again, no matter what.

The next day was bright and clean and clear. They could see the snow-covered peaks of the San Bernardino Mountains in the east. Dan drove to the airport with the top down on their little car, watching the wind as it blew Lilly's blonde hair across her pretty face.

At the airport he stood and waved, watching her plane growing smaller and smaller until it was just a tiny bright spot in the sky. Then she was gone. He stepped away from the fence and turned his face to the war.

Chapter Four

The first Med-Cap had gone well and Dan was writing a letter to Lilly.

Steve stepped into the plywood, tin roofed hootch they were using for an office and said, "The place where we had the Med-Cap was bombed."

Dan said, "What the hell?"

"Yeah, sixty people were killed or wounded."

Dan felt terrible, somehow responsible. He sensed Steve felt the same way. Steve said, "The Doctor's not coming with us anymore."

"Why's that?"

"I don't know, Steve said, "Maybe he's afraid or maybe he just doesn't want to waste his life out there. It's hard to tell. Maybe he feels like it's hopeless."

Dan said, "Maybe it's for the better. I'd rather not deal with someone who doesn't want to be there. It'll just be trouble down the line."

"What about the Corpsmen?"

"They're in."

"Good, I'm gonna go check the mail."

The mail was the lifeline to everything good and decent, everything familiar and safe. Dan knew he was the luckiest guy in Vietnam because Lilly wrote him a letter every day. On the days the mail couldn't get through, he knew there was a letter somewhere on its way and that it would be there the next day or the day after that. Sometimes the knowing was almost as good as the getting.

Many of the guys never got a letter from anybody. Some got "Dear John" letters, then walked around for days trying to understand, or they just got drunk and stayed that way.

There was a letter from Lilly that day. Dan wanted to be alone with it and his thoughts of her. He went to his hootch and sat on the steps in the shade of the banana tree. He opened the envelope and went straight to the "I love you" at the bottom. For now, nothing else mattered.

He thought about the first time they had met. He was at Avila Beach with a group of friends, sitting in the sun watching, the waves when someone doused him with a cup of cold water. Surprised, he turned around to see a pretty brown-eyed blonde with fabulous legs in a blue checked bikini, holding the dripping paper cup and looking at him with a smile.

"Why'd you do that?" He asked.

"You were ignoring me."

He didn't know what to say.

She cocked her head and smiled at him.

Looking into her eyes, he felt like he had known her forever.

Chapter Five

The Bo De (Buddhist) School was on the west side of Highway One, almost a mile up the road from the bombed out provincial office.

Steve was suffering from a headache, so Dan took the truck and went on his own. Looking like it belonged on a farm somewhere, the stake-bed International was the most unmilitary vehicle Dan could imagine. It rattled and banged with each bump in the road. A small sign announcing Yan Su Vu (Civic Action) hung slightly cockeyed where he had wired it to the front bumper.

It was a little cooler today, and the breeze from the side vent windows and the sweat evaporating from his body made the heat almost bearable. He'd also un-bloused his trousers, cut off his shirt sleeves, gave up wearing underwear, and traded his leather boots for a pair of jungle boots.

He slowed to enter the school grounds. There was an abandoned narrow-gauge railroad track from the French occupation running parallel to the road. The truck's tires hit the iron rails and stopped. Dan shifted into low and eased her on over the tracks entering the schoolyard through a worn iron gate. There was a row of single-story classrooms on each side. Evidence of a previous Civic Action presence, a rusty swing-set leaned against the fence next to the gate. A two-story building stretched across the rear of the compound, with broad concrete steps ascending from the schoolyard to a large covered veranda.

Two men were waiting on the steps. One wore the robes of a Buddhist priest, and the other was dressed in a neat short-sleeved white shirt and dark trousers. As Dan walked across the schoolyard, the man in the white shirt stepped down to make the introductions.

Dan reached out to shake hands. Instead of shaking, the man in the white shirt leaned forward in a crisp, almost formal, bow. His hands were pressed together, fingertips pointing upward as in prayer. He was slightly built with carefully trimmed dark hair and intense, intelligent, black eyes.

Rising, he took Dan's hand in both of his and said, "Good morning, Sir. Welcome to the Bo De School. I am Ong De."

He was immaculately clean, and his English was accented, but confident and precise. His eyes never left Dan's. Gesturing toward the man in the robes of a priest, Ong De said, "This is Chaplain Hu."

Chaplain Hu stood on the steps, black falcon eyes flashing with what Dan imagined to be the staggering responsibilities of overseeing both the school and orphanage.

He didn't know if the Buddhists had a warrior class or not, but if they did, Dan believed that Chaplain Hu would be at the head of the column. The priest stood perfectly erect, watching each child and teacher, focused on every detail, as if he were holding the school together by the sheer force of his will.

The priest stepped down and took Dan's hand. He sincerely thanked him for coming. "Cam On," then in accented, careful English, "Thank you to come."

Ong De led Dan to a covered veranda on the left side of the two-story building that sat at the back of the school compound. It was cool and quiet with woven wicker sofas and chairs with comfortable cushions and a low table. Ong De sent one of the pigtailed orphan boys on an errand and motioned for Dan to sit down.

"Please join me for tea."

They smiled at each other across the low table and waited until the boy came back with the tea.

"Cam on." (Thank you) Dan thanked him in Vietnamese and somewhere behind Ong De's keen black eyes there was a flicker of appreciation for the effort. Ong De seemed to be in his late thirties or early forties. Dan was in his early twenties and just out of the university.

Dan asked, "Please tell me about the Bo De School."

Ong De turned in his chair and pointed to the low building on the north side of the compound.

"Primary school." He turned back to Dan and smiled. "The little ones! The other side is the high school, and this building is the orphanage, the kitchen, and what you might call offices. My room, upstairs, is also my home."

"Your family?"

"My mother and father are in Saigon. No wife, no child."

Dan wondered but didn't ask.

Ong De smiled and gestured toward the playground. "These are all my children."

Dan looked around the veranda, the schoolyard and buildings. The students were in class. There were several bicycles leaning against the wall. The calm order of the school felt like an oasis of sanity and order in the midst of a people torn and scattered by decades of chaos.

Dan said, "This is so peaceful, this school, this place."

Ong De smiled broadly. "Chaplain Hu is..."

He paused, searching for the correct English word. "Responsible, responsible for all."

Dan nodded.

Ong De continued, "I am the..." Again he searched for the correct word.

Dan sipped his tea. He was in no hurry. A part of him could sit on this veranda sipping tea forever. Somehow, a part of him had always wanted to be in this place.

Ong De bowed his head and said, "I am what you might say, the headmaster."

The school was Buddhist but Ong De looked more like a teacher or businessman.

"Are you also Buddhist?"

"No."

Dan looked at him wondering.

Ong De smiled and opened his hands. "There is truth in all things."

Chapter Six

The stuff of war. Flare rounds going up and out, opening into the night with a "pop." Strange white light drifted down herky-jerky on a little parachute. Random rockets struggled to reach the ammo dump and fell short into nearby villages. Medivac choppers dripping blood carried dead and wounded Marines to First Med.

Civic Action stopped. No one was allowed to leave the base. Dan and Steve stood extra watches and slept in the mortar trenches.

After several days, the fighting went somewhere else, and the needs of what passed for normal life rose again to the surface. Steve had another headache and was not able to go anywhere. Dan wanted to see what was going on in the village, so as soon as they opened the base he decided to go out by himself.

He had just finished gassing up the truck when Michael Peacock, the battalion photographer, asked, "I was wondering if I could go out to the village with you. I would like to get some shots of the people."

Dan appreciated that Michael wasn't afraid of going "out there" with him and was pleased to have him along.

"I'm going to the Buddhist school. Come along. Steve can't make it. I could use the company."

"How is Steve?"

"The headaches are getting worse and worse."

At the Bo De School, Ong De met Michael and Dan as they came through the gate. Michael was gracious and considerate as Dan introduced him to Ong De. But this time there were no smiles. Ong De called to a young schoolgirl who was wearing the white headband of mourning. She walked slowly to his side, her little sister clinging to her hand.

The girl stood silent, without expression. Ong De gently introduced her as Do Ti Thuan, a fourth grader at the school.

Ong De explained that during the confusion of the fighting her father had been killed. Assassins had come, taken her father out of their home, and shot him in the head. No one said it was the Viet Cong. They never used the term. But the timing and the formality of the execution made it seem that was the case.

Hurt and bewildered, Do Ti Thuan never moved or changed her expression. She seemed to be standing alone, staring into the sudden, grim, uncertain future of a life with no father.

Ong De looked down at the two small girls by his side.

"It is too hard for her mother to keep her in school now." He said, "Her family is too poor. They have no money now that father is killed. She must work to help her family."

"But she's so small. What can she do?"

"Maybe help mother with brother and sister. No father. Everyone in family must work now."

He paused and looked at Dan. "She good student. She try hard."

Helpless, Dan knelt in front her. Her face stamped with grief, she stared over his shoulder at something he could not see. Dan realized that no matter what he did now, the day would come when he would return to the beaches of California and she would stay here, condemned to a life he could not imagine. He rose to his feet and looked at Ong De.

"What can we do?"

Ong De shrugged, shook his head, and gently touched the child's hair. He looked at Dan, his eyes full of sadness and frustration, his almost perfect English undermined by his grief. Dan waited with Ong De and the two girls who seemed so small against the inchoate face of the war.

Ong De spoke quietly with a small sliver of hope. "She can go to school for twenty-five dollars." He paused, "All year."

Dan glanced at her little sister, lost, sad, and afraid. Ong De nodded. "Her too, she is small."

Michael was quiet on the way back to the base. All he said was, "I'll have some photos for you when I get them developed."

Days went by. He wrote Lilly, sharing his sadness and helplessness. Twenty-five dollars didn't seem like much but his pay from the Navy was next to nothing, and almost all of it went to support Lilly while he was gone.

It was still there on his heart when one evening he joined a group of the battalion's truck drivers at the back of the chow line. They were laughing and swapping stories. One big trucker was telling how he had bumped this old papa-san into the ditch with the front fender of his truck.

"Ass over handlebars! You should have seen him fly!"

Everyone laughed but Dan. He didn't think it was funny. That kind of thing wouldn't go unnoticed in the village and could put him at risk when he was out there by himself. Besides, they were supposed to be assisting these folks, not bouncing them off the road like some life-sized pinballs.

He was disgusted, but it didn't seem like that there was anything he could do. He didn't know how to handle it, but he wasn't about to let it go either.

The truckers were not going to appreciate their "fun" being ruined by him pointing out that elders are revered in Vietnam and that an "accident" like that could be fatal to the old man.

He needed to talk to his friend. The next morning he went to the school. Ong De bowed and took Dan's hands in his own. Dan smiled and bowed in turn. He was pleased to see him, this man he admired so much for the way that he somehow seemed to always find a way to rise above the war's constant devastation. How did he find the strength? What did it cost him, no wife, no children, no family of his own?

Ong De motioned toward the welcome shade of the veranda. They sat and waited for the tea, chatting easily across the low table. They used some English and some Vietnamese, warming up their use of both languages, seeking that common place of understanding. One of the teachers brought the tea and placed it with practiced grace on the table. It was just slightly cooler than the heat of the day.

Dan told him about the trucker hitting the old man on the bicycle.

Ong De leaned forward, listening.

"He did it on purpose," said Dan, "and then thought it was funny."

Disgusted, he exhaled, with the realization that he was becoming ashamed of his own country, his own race.

Ong De was listening carefully. "We cannot change him, can we?

Dan shook his head.

Ong De poured tea for Dan and then for himself. "We cannot help the elder either. If he did survive, he may die before too long."

He paused and set the teapot on the table then looked at Dan.

"We must think of today. We must think of Do Ti Thuan and her little sister."

Dan looked at him, confused.

Ong De looked at his hands then across the table.

"Perhaps you can ask the big truck driver for the money to help her stay in school. Maybe now he feels bad inside, like you."

"Maybe." Dan shook his head. "Like a scholarship program of some kind?"

Ong De nodded thoughtfully. "Perhaps. That could be a good thing. There are too many children that need help to go to school."

While he was still at the school, Ong De's suggestion almost made sense. However, by the time he got back to the base it seemed pretty far-fetched.

That same night the truckers were standing outside the chow hall as usual. Even though he had his doubts, Dan could see a flicker of wisdom in Ong De's suggestion. The truck drivers already thought he was some sort of "gook lover" so what did he have to lose?

He joined them at the chow line. They stopped their talking, story telling and laughing.

Dan looked at the big trucker who had bumped the papa-san ass over the handle bars and asked, "You guys want to buy a scholarship for the children at the Bo De School?"

They stared at him like he was talking some language they didn't understand. He took a quick breath and went on. "For twenty-five bucks you can help a child go to school all year."

"A whole year?" They sounded impressed, or maybe starting to feel a little guilty, or maybe hoping he would go away. He didn't.

"Uh huh, twenty-five dollars."

In some sort of internal negotiation with themselves, they nodded and grunted and shuffled their feet. Finally, the big trucker looked around at the other guys, crossed his arms and leaned forward. "Sounds like a good deal. Do I get to meet the little fella?"

Dan had to smile. "You bet. I'll take you down to the school myself."

So that was it. Ong De was right. Following the big trucker's lead, they all bought a scholarship. They even seemed happy about it. Before it was over, the Dentist, Intelligence Officer, Photographer's Mate, and even the crusty old Executive Officer, had purchased scholarships.

The first chance he got he drove down to the school to tell Ong De the news.

Ong De poured the cup of tea and pushed it across the table to Dan. He seemed pleased, but not especially surprised.

Dan was still trying to understand. This chain of events began with the old man being hit by the truck. Now it seemed like it had turned out the way it was supposed to all along. It seemed like another of the strange, random occurrences that were happening all around him. But how could Ong De have seen it, been aware of its possibility?

He remembered him saying, *Maybe now he feels bad inside, like you. Perhaps your feelings are becoming connected.*

On the day of the ceremony the sponsors all stood together on the steps of the school to present the scholarships. Peacock quietly took the photos that documented the event. The big trucker stood head and shoulders above everyone. His arm was around the "little fella" he had sponsored and there was a big smile on his face.

Except for Do Ti Thuan, everyone was smiling.

Chapter Seven

While he was still stateside at Port Hueneme, Dan had heard returning SeaBees say, "In 'Nam, wood is gold." Once he was in country, he learned what it meant. One of the consequences of the war was to deprive the villagers of the charcoal they needed to cook their food. The charcoal came from the hardwood forests, which were controlled by the guerrillas.

Bamboo was everywhere, but it doesn't burn. So when the people did have food, they often had no way to cook it. Desperate, they would dash into a minefield or leap onto the back of a moving truck for a scrap of two-by-four they could use to cook their food or sell on the black market.

With the flood of refugees, the number of children at the Bo De School had increased. So had the need for the benches they used for desks. The Seabees had lumber.

To take a load of lumber to the Bo De School, Dan and Steve had to pass through an area where the shanties crowded in on both sides of the narrow road. Also, there was an intersection where they had to stop and make a left turn. They knew if they weren't careful, their truck could be stripped of its precious load in a matter of minutes.

Steve was driving. Dan sat on the back of the flat bed with the wood. He stuck his head around the cab and yelled, "Keep this thing movin' Steve. Don't stop no matter what. Just keep 'er rollin'!"

But, it did no good. Graceful as matadors, a fellow from each side of the road darted in front of the truck, sliding past the front fenders like the horns of a bull. Steve hit the brakes and stopped. The crowd swarmed the truck. Dan fought them for every stick of wood, but as soon as he grabbed one end of a 2x4 or 2x6, they would take one from the other side.

Finally, he was holding on to one last, lonely 2x6. Two smiling Vietnamese men were on the other end. It was pretty much a standoff. Steve hadn't moved the truck at all. Dan thought about cranking off a round in the air with his forty-five but somehow it just didn't seem worth it for one 2x6.

"Move the damn truck!" yelled Dan, but Steve sat, frozen to the spot.

The two fellows on the other end of the 2x6 were grinning at him while everyone else was enjoying the entertainment. Even while they were robbing him blind, they were unfailingly polite.

Dan finally got tired of looking so damn foolish, said to hell with it, and let go of the 2x6. The truck was picked clean. They finally started moving except they didn't have a load so they had nowhere to go.

After driving around for a while, they decided to go back to the base and write some letters home.

The next time they had a load of lumber, Dan took the keys and said, "I'll drive."

Steve didn't argue.

Rolling down the hill, Dan could see the crowd waiting for them. Pinching in from both sides, the bandits were prepared to force them to stop so they could swarm the truck and strip it like before.

He slammed the transmission into second and floored it. The engine roared. The truck lumbered forward, sideboards rattling and banging. The crowd of bandits held their ground, crowding both sides of the road, ready to pounce.

"Hang on!" he yelled out the window to Steve, then started weaving the truck from one side of the narrow road to the other like he was either drunk or crazy. Slipping the clutch and revving the motor, the old International sounded like a freight train. He turned the wheel and aimed the big truck directly at the crowd on the right side of the road. Their eyes got bigger and bigger. They froze, then gave way. Cranking the wheel, he aimed straight for the crowd of bandits on the left. They fled. The road was open.

He never hit anybody and, from then on, the road stayed open for the crazy drivers in the International flatbed with the red "Yan Su Vu" sign flapping away on the front bumper. They had a clear road and didn't lose any more lumber or anything else.

In the whole scheme of things, it probably didn't matter that much. It was just a matter of pride not to give up their load to a bunch of bandits. He and Steve had to learn how to do their jobs, regardless of the circumstances.

But it seemed as if Steve had less to say every day. They had never really talked about their girls or things like that, and Dan realized that he really didn't know him very well. Although Steve kept on doing his job, it seemed as if he were struggling to make sense of this whole thing and it was wearing on him.

One morning Dan found Steve in the office with his head on the desk.

"What's up man?"

Steve groaned in pain. "My head, it's killing me."

Dan left him and went up to the sick bay. He found Chief Corpsman Critchett and asked, "What's wrong with Steve?"

"He's having horrible headaches. It could be encephalitis."

Dan was stunned. "What's that?"

Chief Critchett stopped what he was doing and looked at Dan, "It's an infection of the fluid between the brain and the skull. The headaches are so bad because the infection causes the fluid to swell until it slowly crushes the brain and kills the person."

Dan was stunned.

The Chief went on. "It's similar to malaria, except much more painful and dangerous, even fatal. He's being Medevac'd to Japan as soon as we can."

The next morning, Dan met Steve stumbling out of his hootch, his face all twisted and closed up with the pain. They looked at each other for a second, and then Steve staggered on to the sickbay. Dan sat down on the front steps of his hootch where the banana tree offered some shade from the mid-morning sun. Steve was leaving and he had never really gotten to know him.

Lilly was so far away he couldn't even imagine whether she was sleeping or awake, much less what her life without him was like. Thank God for her letters. They were the anchor that held him in place. He didn't want to worry her, and so he tried to find something good to share with her, but he needed to tell someone about Steve, so he wrote her a letter.

> *In many ways Steve was a much better Seabee than I'll ever be. He was one of those guys who always played*

by the rules. He could be counted on to do the right thing, no matter what. The problem is that over here, nobody knows what the rules are – what the right thing is. It seems like the one time he didn't do the right thing it might have killed him.

We were given these giant orange "malaria pills" we were supposed to take for ten days. But, they caused guys to have really bad, violent diarrhea. I don't know why, but Steve just couldn't bring himself to go through with it, and now he's really sick.

The corpsmen tell me he has encephalitis. They say it is an inflammation of the fluid around the brain and that it could swell until it crushes his brain and kills him. No wonder it hurts so damn much. All I can think about is The Man in the Iron Mask.

He couldn't even say goodbye. He just looked at me and ran to the sick bay holding his head in his hands. I think they took him to Japan.

What happened to him is so random I just can't make sense of it. A little bug you can't even see got inside of him. He is in such pain and so alone with it. It's like no one can help him. We think about the mortars and the rockets and the guns and the knives, but somehow this is worse.

I want you to know that I will do whatever I have to do to get back to you, to be in your arms again. But, everyday now it seems like I am farther and farther away from you. Sometimes the moon seems closer. At least I can see it from here. When I look at the moon I know you see it too, somewhere on the other side of this big ball.

I feel like I am on another planet, some sort of space traveler searching for you. Please believe that no matter what I have to do, I will come back for you.

He signed the letter and looked out toward Da Nang and the South China Sea.

Whatever it took. Whatever it took. Don't drink, don't use drugs, don't mess with the Vietnamese women. Write Lilly a letter as often as he could. That seemed like a good place to start. Whatever it took.

For the first two weeks in country, he had thought of her and little else. But like it or not, his heart was gradually catching up to the rest of him. Little by little, the constant heat and unrelenting anxiety, the strange sounds and smells were leaching through every cell of his body, draining him of everything he had ever known and everything he had ever been.

He looked at the white rings of salt in his fatigues where his sweat had soaked into the faded green fabric and dried. He could see that with each ring, he was slowly becoming more and more a part of this place on the other side of the world. With each ring, "the world" as he had known it drifted farther and farther out of his reach until all he could imagine of America was Lilly on the beach stretching up, reaching out, gently releasing her letter to him like a paper airplane on the wind.

Dan thought about their last night together, and his unspoken promise that he would come back to her no matter what, and her unspoken promise to him that she would be faithful to him, no matter what.

But what would it take to survive this war, this giant tantrum of old men, this deadly drama where nothing was as it seemed?

What price would he have to pay to see her sweet smile, to look upon her beauty, to be in her arms again?

What price would he pay?

What would he have to do to see her again?

Images of the dead and dying, the bleeding, the women and children and old people face down with a mouthful of dirt came to his mind's eye. Images of the enemy, whoever that might be, who would do him harm, who would kill him in this land where he was so far away from her.

Who was this enemy? How would he know them when they came?

Would he tear them apart with his bare hands? Would he hack them into pieces with his K-Bar, with his teeth?

Would he pierce their hearts?

Would he choke the breath out of them until they could breathe no more?

Would he stomp their brains into the dirt?

Would he kill?

Would he break the "Thou shalt not kill" Commandment?

It was too late to wonder, too late to turn back now.

He would do any, or all of the above, and gladly.

God help him.

But what then? How could she ever want him back? If he did survive, would there be anything left of the person he had once been? Would there be anything left that she could still love? How could she love that flaming marshmallow pulled too late from the weenie roast fire, a brittle blackened shell with the too gooey insides?

He wondered about his great-grandfather, who had carried the Battle Flag for the Wisconsin Thirteenth during the Civil War.

He wondered if he had been afraid, angry, lonely, sick and disgusted. Dan had always thought of him walking off to war with his head high and his duty clear in his mind. The old veteran had always been a larger than life hero who had known his duty and did it with clarity, almost a purity of purpose. But brother against brother? Countryman against countryman? Maybe it hadn't been all that clear to him either.

As a child Dan had found his great-grandfather's medal from the Civil War. It was made of steel. The ribbon was almost gone. It looked like the letters had been stamped by hand, *Company C / 13th Wisconsin Volunteer Infantry / 1861 to 1865.*

He remembered reading a letter his great-grandfather had mailed to his wife, Cherokee. He thought about the part where Hobart had described a "scrape" with Confederate soldiers.

> *Sometimes we talk to the rebs across the river. They don't seem much different than our selves. We got into a scrape with a troop of them the other day when they effected a crossing and came upon on us from downstream. We were outnumbered but the shots from their rifles and muskets sailed over our heads without harm. Given their reputations as marksmen I can only figure they meant to end the killing on that day in their own fashion. Our boys did not return the favor.*

So maybe it wasn't so clear for him either. Maybe it never is for the man with the broken commandment on his soul.

Chapter Eight

Steve was gone, and the Battalion wasn't going to replace him. Dan was on his own. He had been frustrated when Steve had stopped the truck and their load of lumber had been stripped. But he hadn't been angry with him.

He had adapted to working with Steve and he would adapt to him being gone. He discovered that in some ways he preferred being on his own. He was relieved not having to think about what someone else would do. He would make the decisions and bear the consequences.

Dan was on his way back to the base from the Bo De School when he saw a gap between the tightly packed shanties. On impulse, he pulled over and stopped. There was a narrow path running west, directly away from the road. It drew him in. Surrendering to his curiosity, he locked the truck, ducked his head, and disappeared into the sea of shanties.

A smiling young boy peered out of an opening in one of the makeshift huts and called, "Hey Batman!"

Surprised, Dan laughed and greeted him in turn.

The boy giggled and waved. Dan waved back.

Near the road the village was swollen with refugees washed to this shore by the currents of another war they had never asked for. Narrow and dusty, the path was bordered on both sides by humble shelters made of roofing tin, plywood and cardboard. Smiling children called to him from the cracks and window openings.

As he walked farther away from the road, deeper into the village, the Catholic and Buddhist, the French and American influences to which he was accustomed, began to change into something different.

The side-by-side shanties gradually started to give way to more permanent homes with room for gardens and bamboo and broad leaf banana trees between them.

Each step revealed a wonder, a small surprise. He became aware of an unmistakably different consciousness that seemed as deep and as vast as the ocean. Asia.

When he left the road he had been so curious, so full of the thrill of discovery that he had plunged in without thinking. Now he realized that even though he was armed, he had crossed a line of no return. He became aware that he could not defend himself, could not make it back to the road should things go bad.

Suddenly alone, suddenly fearful, he stumbled and stopped to look at his feet. Where were they taking him? Why had they stopped? He checked his M16. The magazine was in place, every fifth round a red tipped tracer.

He was alone, no radio. Except for the truck parked by the side of the road, no one would know where he was or how to find him. Go back or go on? His body wanted to turn back to the false security of the road and his truck and the base where he would be surrounded by the white faces that looked and talked like him.

Torn between the safety of the known world and the enchantment of the unknown he felt split down the middle. His fear of death trapped and held him motionless. The secrets of Asia called to him.

Like the sound of the surf at night, the force of his curiosity pulled him in. Fascinated, he continued into the unknown. The noises of the road were gradually replaced by the sounds of the birds in the bamboo and the people talking softly together, the quiet murmur of village life.

There were homes now in place of shanties. There were chickens and gardens. The smells of nuoc-mam fish sauce, the jungle, and the rich fertility of rice fields in the distance filled the thick, warm air. The spices of the Orient offered their charms on a gentle breeze. Asia washed over him with the sweetness of slightly overripe fruit and countless centuries of quiet understanding.

Sounds and odors faded into the background. Sunlight in the trees above separated into the colors of the rainbow that arched over him glittering like a waterfall of light come alive. A cleansing baptism of light and colors washed over and through him. Shimmering colors and gentle sounds filtered down through everything he believed, everything he had been taught, gently surrounding and touching that part of him that he knew to be true.

He stumbled forward, each step surrendering the illusion of separateness he held so dear. Good and evil, life and death, the fear of his own death, were all wiped away by the sudden and certain understanding that life and death truly are one, and the same.

It occurred to him that if indeed life and death are one and the same then he was already dead and had no need to fear the act of dying. In the next moment, in that same step, he was released from the fear of his own death. The path opened before him.

The trail passed a graveyard, gradually curving from the west toward the north. In the middle of the bend he was startled by the sound of quiet rustling in the brush. It seemed like several people were moving carefully toward him from different directions. The fear that had just left him returned with a rush.

He felt their eyes upon him. He wanted to run. He fought the impulse to turn around but didn't want to show his fear. He considered the possibility his M16 would do little good here. He was too far from the road and appeared to be well outnumbered. He was standing in the open with no cover.

He tried to keep his cool and not appear to be afraid. He took a breath and then another. Nothing happened. He kept walking. As the path gradually bent around to the north he was able to see back down the way he had come.

The villagers were carrying and dragging their sick, injured, and wounded through the brush to the side of the trail. Their suffering made his fears seem so foolish. Awed by their plight and humbled by his helplessness he stopped in the middle of the path.

A young man shadowed him off the side of the trail. He wouldn't look at Dan but kept wandering back and forth in what seemed to be a desperate, speechless plea to be noticed.

He had no hair. Instead, his hair had been replaced by a thick layer of infection that had grown between the skin of his scalp and the bone of his skull. It extended from above his eyebrows to the back of his neck and down to his ears on each side.

He was completely bald, and the infection was so thick and misshapen that it looked to Dan as if he were wearing a skin colored football helmet. Other than the horrible affliction, he looked like a normal high school or university student.

An elderly Mama-san held her head in her hands, her jaw swollen from what looked like an infected tooth. Her mouth was dark red, almost black, and her eyes were glazed from the narcotic effects of the betel nut.

Dismayed by their desperate, hopeless circumstances he looked back and forth as they surrounded him. Here, deep in the village, lining the trail with their silent pleas, people carried their sick and wounded to him.

It seemed like a scene from Dante's Inferno, or the Bible. He thought of Jesus as a young man and the incredible burden and heartbreak that he must have faced as the countless sick and lame were brought to him to somehow be healed.

The trail intersected a path coming across the rice field from the west. Surrounded by the sick and injured, he knew that he had found the best place possible to bring the Corpsmen and the miracle of their medicine to these people.

Chapter Nine

Tired and dusty from his day in the village, Dan sat down on the front steps of his hootch and lit one of the unfiltered, king-sized Pall Malls that came with the C-rations. Smith, a friend from one of the builder companies, walked up the hill, leaned his M16 up against the hootch and sat down.

From a small town in rural Georgia that had given him his place in the world, Smith was one of those rare individuals who always had a pretty good idea of what he was doing and why.

He was well muscled, with a round, intelligent face, and blond, curly hair. While he wasn't exactly handsome, he had become the Battalion's "Handsome Sailor." Everyone wanted to confide in him, so he was keenly aware of what was going on. He was one of the few people, at any level, who seemed to understand how it all fit together.

Dan offered him one of his last Pall Malls.

Smith lit it up and sat back. The smell of the first smoke drifted up to Dan. Smith inhaled and said, "Man, these things are like a small cigar."

They smoked in silence for a while taking the smoke and the nicotine rush that came with it. Dan liked the smoking part of it. He just didn't much care for how it made him feel later on.

Smith looked at the Pall Mall. He wasn't much of a smoker either. "I hear there's a bunch of guys out there who've gone AWOL for one reason or another."

Dan shook his head. "I don't understand it."

"Yeah, but let's face it Dan, we've got it made. Most of them ain't so lucky."

"But still, that's pretty radical, man."

Smith shrugged. "Have you seen a newspaper from the states lately?

Dan shook his head. "Just the Stars and Stripes."

Smith grunted and spit a piece of tobacco off the end of his tongue. "Well, almost every major city in the United States of America, the good Ol' US of A, has been, or will be soon, up in flames. Take a look at this."

Smith had the paper folded neatly in his hip pocket. It was the front page of the Atlanta Journal-Constitution. "My folks sent it to me."

Smith handed him the paper. On the front page, there was a map of the U.S. in color, city after city, a broad swath of cities in flame. Dan read it shaking his head. New York, Washington DC, Detroit, Chicago, Los Angeles, all in flame. Kent State, Berkeley, university after university.

Dan was shocked. "What the hell's going on? Looks like the war's at home instead of over here." Dan shook his head and gave the paper back to Smith. "What's going on?"

Smith shrugged, "Sometimes they say it's race riots. Sometimes it's against the war and the draft. Some say it's the Hippies or the long hairs. None of it makes sense to me."

Dan shook his head. "This looks like we're at war with ourselves."

For some reason Dan thought of the funny looking union or confederate hats that were popular with boys when he was in elementary school. Some wore gray but in Iowa, most wore blue.

He asked Smith if he remembered those caps, inspired by some memory of the Civil War.

Smith laughed, "Sure do, but ours were all gray. And it's not the Civil War where I come from. Most people still call it the War of Northern Aggression."

Dan looked at his green fatigue cap in his hands. "I wonder what they will call this mess a hundred years from now?"

Smith looked at him sideways. "They'll forget it as soon as they can, just like they'll forget us, just like those poor fuckers running around out there in the 'ville. It seems to me that those guys are right in the middle of it somehow and don't even know it. Nobody's gonna give a shit about them, or us."

Smith tossed his cigarette butt in the dirt. "Think about it, Dan. They could die out there and nobody's gonna give a shit. Nobody's gonna know. Nobody's gonna be foldin' a flag or blowin' taps for em."

Dan asked, "Why do you think they go AWOL in the first place?"

Smith shrugged and said, "From what I hear, a guy could get in a beef with his command and be looking at some jail time and take off, or have a girl out there somewhere or maybe even a kid. Or maybe they get a Dear John or something and go off the deep end, or maybe they're just sick of this whole fucking thing. They get out there in the ville', Dan, and they can't get back. Take a look at the paper. How many of these guys are even going to have a place to go home to?"

Smith dug a chunk of mud out of the sole of his jungle boot. He looked up, squinting against what was on his mind. "They'll kill you Dan. They'll kill you for your weapon, or your ID or any papers you might have on you."

He pointed at the little Yuan Su Vu, Civic Action badge Dan wore clipped to his shirt pocket. "They would love to have that. You can go anywhere you want with that, right?"

Dan looked down at the badge on his shirt. "Guess I never thought about it."

Smith stood up and poked him on the shoulder. "Watch your step, Seabee. That badge won't stop a bullet."

Dan watched him walk away until he couldn't see him anymore.

He was surprised at how different Smith's life had been from his own and how Smith was very much a son of the antebellum south. Dan thought about how the missions, the gracious, accepting values of the early Californians, the beaches, the mountains and the vastness of the great ocean had all such a profound influence on who and what he was today.

He thought of his great-grandfather leaving his wife and baby boy for four years of war. There were no RnR's, and mail service was uncertain. His great-grandfather had no idea when he would return, if ever. Dan respected the way he had seemed to serve his country without flinching. He admired the way he had carried the battle flag for the Wisconsin 13th and then returned to serve his community as the Constable and Justice of the Peace. He was impressed by the way Hob and Cherokee had raised and canned food to distribute to the destitute widows of the Civil War soldiers who had perished fighting their brothers.

From a distance, Hob's war seemed much simpler than Dan's. However, at that time it must have been confusing and dreadful to bring his weapon to bear on his countrymen in order to liberate the slaves who were equally his countrymen.

Dan wondered if it required that much blood, that much sacrifice, to somehow begin to pay the weight of slavery on the soul of the nation.

He remembered he and Lilly taking the Greyhound bus from Disneyland back to Ventura late one Sunday night and how they had watched the glow from the "Happiest Kingdom" gradually being replaced on the horizon by the light of flames from the riots and burnings in the Watts section of Los Angeles.

The next day, the Battalion had been held on the base all day, and at dusk the men were mustered out in the parking lot. Axe handles had been neatly stacked next to a long line of buses with their parking lights on, diesel engines idling in the near dark, ready to take the men to "knock heads" in the burning city.

Dan had been standing in formation with a vague sense that this was a bad idea and possibly in violation of the Constitution. Finally, he had refused to go, saying to anyone listening, "I'm going home now. If you want me you can come and get me."

He stepped out of formation and drove to the little apartment in Ventura where Lilly was waiting for him with dinner.

Someone, somewhere, must have thought better of it, and the whole thing was called off. It was never mentioned again, like it had never happened.

So what was he doing here now in Vietnam? Who were we fighting and what for? These people were not a threat to the United States. He wondered if his generation was somehow paying for the sin of its fathers, the slave holders, and the slaves.

Dan thought about what Mohamed Ali had so famously said. "I ain't got no quarrel with them Viet Congs. None of them ever called me nigger."

Chapter Ten

Still sitting on the front steps of his hootch, Dan could see the land sloping down toward the villages, the highway and the sea in the far distance. He saw the mail truck speed up the hill and through the front gate. After waiting long enough to let the crowd clear, he stood up, and walked down to the little Post Office.

Hunter, the Battalion Postal Clerk, was behind the counter. He was a big guy with dark hair in a crew cut who wore thick glasses and took his job seriously. He knew something about almost everyone in the Battalion, who was getting mail and who wasn't. He knew who got a Dear John, and who didn't get any mail at all.

He was the men's lifeline to the world, and they watched him every day to see if he was going to make the mail run. He knew they depended on him, so he would take his shotgun and his M1 carbine and go for the mail whenever it was safe and sometimes when it wasn't.

But today he looked troubled and Dan could see that he wanted to talk.

He held on to Dan's letter from Lilly and said, "Can I talk to you about something?"

"Sure."

"Don't know who else to talk to."

Dan didn't say anything.

"It's about the Senior Chief."

Dan didn't especially want to hear about Hunter's problems with the Senior Chief, and besides he wanted to read his letter from Lilly. But Hunter had his letter and Dan could see he wasn't going to hand it over until he had his say.

"Okay."

Hunter took a deep breath.

"Maybe you could talk to someone. You play cards with the Lieutenant and the Chaplain sometimes, don't ya?"

"Sometimes."

"I can't get in any trouble, Dan."

"I understand all about that."

A young Seabee came in hoping for a letter that wasn't coming. He glared at Hunter like it was his fault, then at Dan, like it was his. He left with his head down and his hands in his pockets, kicking the dirt as he went.

"I don't like it Dan. I don't think it's right what the Senior Chief's doing, but I do the mail. I know what's going on, but there's nothing I can say, nothing I can do about it. We have rules, you know, postal rules."

Dan decided it was best to get it over with. "What the hell is going on Hunter?"

Hunter grunted like he was in pain and looked around, "You know about the Pen-Pal program, right?"

"I guess."

Hunter started stammering, just trying to spit it out. "You know, school girls writing to guys overseas to cheer them up – little kids, you know, young girls, girls in grammar school or Junior High."

"Yeah?" Dan couldn't see where this was going but figured that since he got a letter from Lilly every day, Hunter must have figured that he was okay. Hunter looked around to make sure no one was listening.

"The Senior Chief told me to watch for the Pen-Pal letters and give them all to him."

"What for?"

"He acts like he's gonna hand 'em out to the guys who aren't getting any mail or anything, but he's not. He's answering all of the letters by himself. He's pretending to be a lonely young guy over here."

"You're shittin' me."

"Nope, but that ain't all. When they write him back, he starts asking them for their addresses and phone numbers and pictures of themselves in their underclothes or bathing suits or nothing on at all!"

Hunter was upset, raising his voice in a plea for help. "I'm not supposed to know, but I can tell, something's not right."

It occurred to Dan that Hunter must have opened some of the mail when he started to suspect what was going on and was afraid of getting into trouble for it.

"That's fucked up," said Dan, shaking his head.

"He's a bad ol' pervert, Dan. If he finds out I said anything to anybody he'll put it on me, and I'll end up in the brig with no career in the postal service, or in Leavenworth for a long time."

"I'll do what I can, Hunter, but you gotta understand, nobody's gonna wanna to hear this shit."

"I know."

Dan kicked the bottom of the counter with the toe of his jungle boot.

"Someone ought'a stick that son-of- bitch."

Hunter leaned across the counter, handed Dan his letter from Lilly and said, "They'd be doin' us all a favor."

Walking back to his hootch he thought about his first contact with the Senior Chief.

The Battalion was at Camp Pendleton for military training before shipping out to Vietnam. It was 1968 and Pendleton was running full bore. Everyone had been issued heavy leather boots and two pair of socks. The next morning they were mustered out for an early breakfast and a ten-mile hike.

The hike started by first climbing a hill and marching through a creek. The Marines are experts on blisters. They knew that at the end of ten miles the wet boots with two pairs of socks would keep the Battalion's fifteen hundred feet from blistering, and like an old baseball mitt, the boots would dry to an exact fit.

The Seabees didn't march so much as they walked along talking to each other. It wasn't like they didn't try to do the military thing. It just wasn't in them. It was pretty much like they had traded their Levis and Dickies for Marine Corps greens and their hammers and saws for M16's. Dan got the feeling they were all just going from one job site to the next.

Chief Jefferies had joined Dan's squad, walking and talking together up the hill to where the hike began.

"Where are you from Chief?" asked one of the guys.

"San Antone."

Carefully looking at the ground in front of each step, the Chief smiled and said, "A bunch of us were in the reserves there and we got to talking about the war. After a few beers we decided we ought'a get out here an' start doin' our part."

One of the guys asked the question that was on everybody's mind. "You volunteered?"

The Chief looked up and nodded, a broad, genuinely pleased smile breaking the lines of his weathered face. "Yep."

The Chief was square and solid with years of hard work stamped on his face and hands. His uniform hung at odd angles while he seemed to move inside of it. It didn't fit him and never would. Dan could see Chief Jefferies was stiff with pain in his joints from the way he walked, his feet splayed out with each step as he tried to keep up.

The squad slowed a little for him with the genuine respect and unspoken love of men who had spent lifetimes working together on dangerous jobs in difficult locations. Most of them had learned to watch out for each other while acting like they were minding their own business. They sacrificed their bodies to day after day of hard work, while often drinking too much at night to ease the pain.

There was a comfortable silence as they continued up the hill while the morning sun warmed their backs. The trail dropped down to a row of trees beside a creek. They waited a moment for the squad in front of them to walk on through the water and up the bank on the other side.

A jeep with a couple of Chiefs pulled up to the side and stopped. A Senior Chief was driving.

Like anyone, Senior Chiefs come in all shapes and sizes. Ours was skinny with poor posture and the face of a ferret.

Of course, he was a lifer and the word was he was not even a Seabee but had transferred over from the regular Navy.

"Hey Jefferies, wanna ride?"

"No thanks, Chief."

"Come on, ride with us." It was almost an order. The Senior Chief tried to smile as he said it but it came out more like a sneer.

Chief Jefferies looked at the muddy water in front of him. The men waited. "I'm gonna go with these guys, Chief."

"Have it your way, Jefferies!" The Senior Chief said and turned away, disdain, disgust and "you'll regret this" on his face.

He spun the jeep around and gunned it past the men and down the dirt road.

Chief Jefferies and the men watched him go, turned to the front and stepped into the creek together, waiting while the cool water filled their boots.

Now Dan was in country. Pendleton, like the rest of California, was drifting farther away with each day that passed. He sat on the steps to his hootch, wondering why he had the feeling there was some sort of vague connection between the Senior Chief and the bombing at the Med-Cap.

Sure, the Senior Chief was a jerk when they were at Pendleton and in light of the letters from the Pen-Pals, he hadn't gotten any better since they had arrived in country. It was pretty clear that whatever he was into, he was into it for himself. It didn't make sense, but this was the military, with layers and layers of corruption and self-interest. Many things didn't make sense. He wasn't surprised, just wondering.

Dan went up to the sickbay and talked to Bobby. "Why do you think the Senior Chief sent us out there? It just doesn't make sense to blow up the people we're trying to help."

Bobby shook his head. "I don't know what's up with that guy, Dan. He's strange. That's for sure."

Dan shook his head and changed the subject. "I found a great place for the Med-Caps."

Bobby was interested. "Where abouts?"

Dan told him about the intersection of the two trails near the graveyard. He told him about the villagers bringing all the sick and wounded to the side of the trail.

"I have never felt so helpless. Will you go back in there with me?"

Bobby nodded. "Heck ya, sounds perfect!"

Chapter Eleven

He was back in the village where the trails intersected and where the people had brought their sick and injured to the side of the trail. He was back and he had brought the Corpsmen with him. Dan stood in the back of the flatbed International, leaning on the top of the cab as he watched the villagers arriving to see the Bac-shi.

The people stood smiling, patiently waiting their turn. There was no urgency or demand for attention. He could tell they felt safe here. So did he. It had taken awhile, but he'd made it back with the Corpsmen and the medicine, and the flatbed with the Yan Su Vu sign on the front bumper. He watched the corpsmen treating each person with gentle efficiency.

Bobby handed him a gallon jug of purple syrup and a stack of small plastic cups and said, "We call this Purple Magic."

He pointed to the line of children with distended abdomens. "For the worms, give each one a cup."

One small boy stepped forward rubbing his tummy. "Dao boom" (stomachache)

Dan poured the purple liquid into the small plastic cup and handed it over the side of the truck, the boy took it down, handed the cup back to Dan with a big smile and said, "Cam on." (Thank you) It went like that all morning.

He stopped what he was doing and watched Chief Critchett treat the young man with the thick layer of infection under his scalp that looked like a flesh colored helmet. Leaning over the side of the truck he asked the Chief about the prognosis, "What's gonna happen to him?"

Approaching middle age, Art Critchett was tall and slightly stooped from bending over his patients. He was completely fearless and dedicated to the administration of medicine to whoever was in need. He also shared Dan's admiration for Dr. Thomas Dooley. Even though the Battalion Doctor was officially in charge of the medical program, Chief Critchett set the program's standards and goals by his humble dedication to serving each and every soul who came to him for treatment.

He looked up from the young man he was treating and said, "He'll be fine. I gave him an injection of a very mild antibiotic, and applied some antibiotic salve to the scalp. He's got what was left in the tube, and a couple of weeks from now you're not going to be able to tell him from anyone else."

Dan was speechless. It was one of the worst afflictions he had ever seen, and now the young man was going to be okay. The Chief looked at him and chuckled. "The miracles of modern medicine Dan, the miracles of modern medicine."

The mother with the listless baby girl was a different story. The Chief was less optimistic about her prognosis. "We'll do what we can, but she's barely breathing, and not nursing or responding at all."

Dan asked," She was at the last Med-Cap out on the road, wasn't she?"

"Yes she was. We gave her some salve to rub on the soft spot but I'm afraid that was just to make the mother feel better. There really is nothing we, or anybody else, can do. She's just too tiny, and the infection has reached too far into the brain."

The sick and the lame, the injured, wounded and the afflicted, just kept coming. Dan ran out of Purple Magic about the same time the Corpsmen ran out of supplies and called it a day.

Most of the villagers had left but Dan noticed one of the elders waiting patiently by the graveyard. When the Med-Cap was over, he approached Dan and bowed. Dan bowed to him in turn. The older man spoke and one of the boys interpreted.

"He say please to wait. Elders come – talk you."

The Corpsmen were packed up and ready to go, but he could see they weren't going to leave without him.

"You guys can go on. It looks like they want to have a meeting of some kind. I'll see you back at the base."

Bobby looked around. "We can stay."

"You've done your part here, and more. It's okay."

"How do you know?"

Dan grinned at Bobby and shrugged.

"You just saved their lives."

The Med-Cap had been successful and safe. It seemed like the farther he was from the road and the base, the safer he felt. Here, where the two trails came together near the graveyard, it seemed to Dan that the villagers' ancestors were looking on in silent approval.

While he was waiting, a young girl hurried down the trail, her bare feet skimming quickly over the smooth, dusty ground. She carried a long bamboo pole over her shoulder with a five-gallon can of water hanging just above the ground on each end. When she could bear the weight no longer, she stopped and lowered her shoulder a little, resting the weight of the water on the earth. She paused briefly, gave Dan a big smile, and then stepped forward into her load, already moving smoothly along the trail.

The other elders arrived and Dan greeted each one with a bow. They smiled, greeted him, and bowed in turn. He could see they had talked among themselves and had come to a decision that involved him. Through the boy acting as an interpreter, they said, "Please come."

Walking quietly together through the curious village, they followed the trail north past humble homes with carefully tended gardens. Leaving the trail, they stepped to the edge of a clearing that opened onto the central rice field.

On the other side was part of the village where he had never been. There were two hamlets, one directly across the field and another tapering away south and west toward the distant hills.

He could see some small shrines on the other side. Because he had been working at the Buddhist school, he assumed these people were also Buddhist. Thinking of Chaplain Hu, he said, "I would like to meet with your priests."

Through the boy interpreting, the elders said, "We have no priests."

Thinking they did not understand, Dan asked them again to meet with their priests. Again, they said they had none. Confused, he gestured toward the small shrines and said, "I see the shrines. I don't understand."

They spoke quietly among themselves, and then nodding together, they patiently explained, "We have no priests."

He still didn't understand. They paused, regrouped and went on, the boy speaking slowly, "Each father is priest. Each home is shrine."

Dan stood silently. For some reason he thought of the Bible verse that says to "pray without ceasing."

He touched the engraved brass bracelet that he had been given by Chaplain Hu and his friends at the Bo De School. It had made him feel accepted and safe and honored. Now he was being invited to enter another world. Looking out across the field of rice he began to understand what they were trying to share with him.

Dan could see that every part of their life, each handful of soil, each grain of rice, each child, each smile was sacred. Looking west, across the rice field to the bamboo forests and their homes on the other side, he felt he belonged here, at home, and at peace, in this quiet, distant place.

Ten thousand years of the Tao, Confucius, the Buddha of China and the Buddha of India, the Hindu and the Cao Dai, planted with patience, a harvest of wisdom. Protected by their isolation, blessed by their ancestors, they shared an easy, timeless harmony in the bamboo forests and rice fields, each generation gently cradling the ones to come with those who had gone before.

Chapter Twelve

He had been told that his job was to support the local government in any way he saw fit. He was given a truck and a badge that allowed him to go anywhere he wished. He thought about Conrad and Lord Jim, except now he was not reading about Asia in a book. He was living in an Asian village with a people who had accepted and protected him.

This was his job. His assignment, his duty, the people and the problems they faced were real. The Viet Cong, the deserters, the warlords and criminal gangs were real. The corruption of the Senior Chief and his cronies was real. American cities were now being put to the torch at the same time as the bamboo huts in Vietnamese villages. From what he could see, his countrymen didn't know, and didn't want to know, anything about the Vietnamese whose beloved homeland they had invaded, occupied and were destroying.

How could he know if he was doing more harm than good to these people who were so vulnerable? How long before he caved in to his own needs? How long before the war swept them all away? Thank God for his friend Ong De and the elders who led him through the lessons of each day. And thank God for Lilly and the letter she was mailing somewhere today.

Taking a break from the heat of the day, Dan and the village men had settled back into the shade of the bamboo at the edge of the rice field. While they were talking, a young American soldier came out of the bamboo forest on the other side. He was bare headed and didn't appear to have a weapon. They watched him walk slowly toward them, looking from side to side as if he were disoriented or looking for someone.

Half way across the field a young boy was napping on the back of a water buffalo. The soldier approached the boy and Dan could see them talking. After a moment the soldier moved on, and the boy slipped off the back of the buffalo and came running to his father.

Someone quickly translated for Dan, "He have hand grenade." The boy made the motion of pulling the pin and said, "No pin. He want woman."

Dan didn't know what to think. Nothing had prepared him for this. He stepped out from under the shade of the bamboo and the young soldier stopped. Surprised to see an American, he quickly turned north and began running up the field away from Dan and the elders. One of the men lived in that direction with his wife and daughter. Unarmed, he jumped on an old bicycle and began pedaling furiously up the trail through the bamboo, his short-sleeved white shirt and white cotton hat briefly visible through gaps in the forest.

Dan picked up his M16, inserted a magazine, pulled back the bolt and watched the red tipped tracer round slide into the black chamber. He and the other men followed the American's tracks up the field, the cries and shouts of the women calling to them from the forest, marking the deserter's every step. Then it was silent.

A woman screamed and the yelling started up again. Turning into the bamboo they followed the noise to the home where the father's bicycle had been left on the ground. The other villagers had gathered around the clearing, chattering together. The women were chastising the deserter, scolding and telling him what they thought of him in no uncertain terms.

The father was standing by the doorway of his home talking quietly to someone inside. He saw Dan and the men and motioned with his hand for them to stay back. Dan moved around the clearing until he could see through the doorway. The room was dark and the American boy sat on the floor with his back to the wall. One hand held the grenade and with the other he had hold of the girl. Her garment was ripped and her breasts were exposed. She was motionless.

Ong Bey and the other PF's joined them. One of the boys had an M16 with extra magazines in a cloth sling around his neck. The rest carried M1 carbines. The other villagers had gathered around the clearing, chattering together.

The girl's father stood by the door. He looked at Dan. Dan looked at Ong Bey. Ong Bey grunted, "He hungry."

Dan stepped toward the door and tried to make eye contact with the GI. The boy's eyes were wide and unfocused. The skin of his face was drawn tight. He sat staring straight ahead holding the frightened girl with one hand and the little green ball of death in the other. It had gotten very quiet. Everyone was waiting on him. He had no idea what to say or do. He stepped back, trying to put some distance between himself and the grenade.

He looked at Ong Bey. The old soldier wasn't smiling. He said, "Numba ten GI."   (American deserter)

Dan guessed that because the deserter was an American, Ong Bey intended for him to take the lead. Stepping closer he took out his last Pall Mall, lit it, and asked "What's your name?"

The boy's eyes focused on the cigarette. He said, "Boyle."

"You hungry, Boyle?"

"Huh?"

"You hungry? You want something to eat?"

Dan inhaled then blew out the smoke from the cigarette.

Boyle said, "I'll take one of those Pall Malls."

Dan held it out toward him and said, "Last one."

He could tell that Boyle wanted the cigarette but didn't know what to do to get it. The onlookers who had gathered around the doorway were quiet, watching and waiting.

Boyle let go of the girl and struggled to his feet. He stepped toward the door with his eyes on the Pall Mall.

The girl pulled her clothes around herself and slid across the floor to her mother. The father watched from the doorway and then backed away to let Boyle through.

Boyle came to the door, held out the grenade and asked, "What do I do with this?"

His hands were shaking.

"Do you have the pin?"

He shook his head back and forth. "No. No pin."

Dan looked at Ong Bey. He and the PF's were moving everyone back out of the way leaving a clear path to the rice field.

The mother and the daughter went out the back of the house where the father joined them.

Dan turned to Boyle and asked, "Do you remember infantry training, when you had to throw one of those things?"

Boyle nodded slowly.

"Remember how they said to hold it tight and not drop it?"

He nodded again.

Dan said, "Okay. You and I are going to walk slowly and carefully toward the rice field where you can get rid of it so no one gets hurt. Can you do that?"

Boyle looked around. It was just the two of them now; everyone else had backed away. He nodded and stepped through the door. He and Dan walked out from under the shade of the bamboo into the heat of the sun. Dan stopped and motioned for Boyle to step in front of him.

"Are you ready?"

Boyle looked at Dan and shook his head. "I don't know. I don't know what will happen."

"What do you mean?"

Boyle looked at the villagers watching from the bamboo. "Those VC will kill me."

"They're not VC, and they're not going to kill you. They're not very happy with you right now, but those are some of the most civilized folks you'll ever meet."

Boyle turned his head to look at Dan. Dan looked him in the eye and said, "Okay, let's take care of that grenade. Remember infantry school? Get a good grip, throw it as far as you can, and then hit the dirt."

He gave Dan a blank look. "That's what my instructor said."

"And how did it work out?"

"Good."

"Good. Then let's do it just like that."

Boyle threw the grenade, and Dan dropped to the ground. Wham! He felt the hard concussion from the grenade through the ground.

Boyle had fallen forward with the throw and was on the ground, sobbing into the dirt. Dan sat beside him and waved to the people to let them know they could go about their business. He wasn't sure, but he thought Ong Bey was smiling.

Chapter Thirteen

Dan went to pick up his mail. Hunter wasn't talking. Dan imagined he was upset about the Senior Chief and the Pen Pals. He figured that if Hunter complained to anyone in command the Senior Chief would see to it that he could forget a career in the Navy or the Postal Service.

Yeah, the good ol' Senior Chief. Dan had noticed that the Senior Chief had developed a sort of following, a gang of four to five guys, sometimes more, hanging around his office at the main gate. Durwood, a guy who bunked in Dan's hootch, was usually with them.

One night everyone was in their bunks, and some of the guys started talking about their first sexual experiences. Dan placed his hands under his head and looked out through the screen into the dark. He thought about some of the girls he had known, but didn't feel inclined to share. His thoughts of Lilly were tucked away in a safe place in his heart.

Then Durwood said, "I bet you can't beat this."

No one said anything.

"I bet you never did it to a mule."

Silence. Durwood went on. "There was this farmer outside of town who had a mule with a tin can nailed to a post beside the stall. You could drop a quarter in the can, and when that old mule heard the tin can go 'Clink,' it would back right up to the end of the stall so you could do your business right there."

No one laughed or said a word, but Durwood went on. "Hell, sometimes I fooled that old farmer and just rattled the can to save myself a quarter!"

Durwood was right. No one could top it. Dan was amazed. Not only was Durwood admitting to bestiality, he was actually bragging about it.

That was the end of the conversation. Dan turned to the wall and tried to clear his mind.

Whump! The sound of the mortar crew firing an illumination round was a welcome interruption. The light from the flare reflected off the plywood walls inside the hootch. Dan looked around the room. Except for Durwood, everyone had turned away, facing the wall. Durwood looked like he was asleep. Dan didn't care to imagine what his dreams might be. The flare went out. It was dark.

Whump! Another flare went up. He was glad someone was paying attention. He went to sleep thinking about being at the beach with Lilly. He dreamed about the water and the waves, the gentle irresistible feeling of the effervescent surf tingling against his skin, tumbling him scrubbed clean to where she waited for him on the shore.

Chapter Fourteen

There was a letter from Lilly waiting for Dan but he never got it. As he was walking down the hill to the post office, the air above him was torn into the silent scream of metal ripping the sky into pieces. A 122mm long-range rocket plowed into the earth next to him and exploded. The concussion picked him up and hurled him through the air. Time slowed until he felt like he was in some sort of never-ending car wreck. He landed face down in the dirt with his arms around his head.

When he looked up the air was full of books. The rocket had landed behind a big wooden box full of books that had protected him from the shrapnel. Now the books were in the air, falling slowly, pages gently flapping like doves descending to evening water.

He watched a book fluttering through the air. It landed in front of him with the pages spread, Henry Wadsworth Longfellow. Without moving from where he had landed, Dan began reading the Longfellow but couldn't remember what he had read.

Wham! Another rocket landed farther down the hill. Wham! Another and another, Wham! Each concussion reached back up the hill through the earth, found him, kicked him in the guts, lifted him off the ground and slammed him back down. He tried to dig in with his fingers and toes but it didn't do any good. He decided not to take it personally and that seemed to help.

Wham! Wham! More rockets, now moving down the hill and east, away from him, seeking the ammo dump, just out of range.

His squad leader ran up, leaned over and pointed at the machine gun tower on the southeast corner of the perimeter. He yelled something as he ran off but Dan couldn't hear what he said.

A machine gun tower, what a truly bad idea. Dan pressed as close to the earth as he could get. He didn't want to be in any tower sticking up in the air. He wanted the earth around him. He wanted to find a hole and crawl into it.

One of the Corpsmen ran by, "You okay?"

Dan couldn't hear but nodded his head that he was. The Corpsman eyeballed him and ran on. He wanted nothing more than to lie there and take a nap, but since he had told the Corpsman he was Okay, he figured he should act like it.

He tried to stand up. He was dizzy, but everything seemed to be working and he wasn't bleeding anywhere except from his nose and ears. He couldn't hear but remembered he was supposed to report to the machine gun tower. Ears still ringing, he wandered in the general direction until he found it.

Climbing the ladder, step by step, he thought, this would make a truly great tree house.

Leaky, tired looking sand bags covered the floor. A few were stacked part way up the wall. It looked like they had been there for a while and he suspected there weren't enough of them to do much good. He figured the Battalion had been taking it easy for too long. Now it was too late to do anything about it. The squad leader pointed at the M60 machine gun, "Your turn Dan."

Dan stared at it. He couldn't move. What the hell? Things were getting serious. Would he kill someone with that thing? Someone he didn't even know? Someone fighting for their country, their home, their loved ones? Would he pull the trigger when the time came? He couldn't imagine it.

The squad leader was waiting, pointing at the gun, impatient. Dan couldn't put it off any longer. It was against everything he had ever been taught, everything he believed. Now, his life was being drawn through a knothole in the graveyard fence to this moment.

There was no way out. He sat down behind the gun. It possessed the unmistakable scent of the orderly, precise world of machine shops and factories where skilled men with educated hands knew exactly what they were doing, and why. It glowed with the confidence of a freshly cleaned and oiled weapon.

He touched the butt of the gun, carefully placing his finger inside the trigger guard.

Call me Mr. Cool.

The M60 was talking to him.

Mr. Cool?

Yeah, do you like the name?

Sure.

Mr. Cool chuckled.

Shoot much?

Just jackrabbits and ground squirrels when I was a kid.

This isn't much different. Short bursts — tuk-tuk-tuk. Keep the barrel down — tuk-tuk. Make the bad guys, jump. Get 'em on the run and cut 'em down — tuk-tuk-tuk. Look for their muzzle flash and watch the tracers. Ours are red, theirs are green. If the green ones start com'n back at ya, let 'er rip!

Dan looked at the long barrel and the belt of 7.62 NATO rounds feeding the gun. He forgot about the other guys in the tower. It was just Dan and the gun.

He sighted out along the long, well-oiled barrel and waited.

Scared?

Dan fingered the trigger gently.

No, not so much. Not with you around. I just don't want to look bad in front of the other guys.

Mr. Cool chuckled again.

Don't worry kid. This is what I'm good at. Just watch the tracers. I'll follow your lead and take care of the rest. Once those rounds start reaching out there, everything changes. Just lean back and let me do my thing – tuk-tuk-tuk. It's a party, my boy, just a party.

The Tet Offensive had started with the rockets. Now it was dark and the show began in earnest. Although he didn't like being up in the gun tower, Dan could see that he had the best seat in the house. Like Mr. Cool said, it was a party.

Whump! Ears still ringing like he was underwater, Dan heard the first illumination round leave the mortar pit. Pop! The chute opened high above and the flare drifted down in the strange flickering light of an old black and white movie.

A flare ship circled high above, flares slowly drifting lower, and lower, finally flickering out and suddenly it was dark, dark everywhere. The only color was the red and green lines of the tracer rounds streaking through the night with deadly intention. He held his breath until another chute opened. It was light again! The flare ship droned on.

Helicopter gunships circled, door gunners firing like they knew what they were shooting at. Converted DC3s the guys called "Spookys", or "Puffs", circled slowly, seemingly supported in the air by the solid columns of tracer rounds from their Gatling guns drilling into the ground. Propeller-driven Skyraiders strafed the earth into neat gardens of leaden rows.

Dark, Dark, Dark again! Damn it! Where were the flares?

Whump! – Whump! Whump! Pop! Pop, Pop – illumination rounds up high. It was light. He released the breath he had been holding.

The Marines were putting up flares too. It wasn't dark but it wasn't light either. Everything was black and white, the flares swinging back and forth on their little chutes, making everything move around while they dropped closer and closer to the ground, the light getting dimmer and dimmer as one by one they were snuffed out as the night's rushing darkness flooded back to its rightful place.

He was staring into the dark but couldn't see any NVA. From the firing, it looked like they were somewhere in the rice field between him and the village out in front of the base. Maybe they were on the dark, overgrown hillside to his right.

A mortar went "Whump" in the tube again and then "Pop" high above. The parachute opened and the flare lit up the night again in the strange glare of a nasty dream that he wanted to wake up from, but couldn't.

Little figures in black pajamas moved through the brush on the hill outside the perimeter! He swung the barrel in that direction while his finger searched for the trigger guard!

Something's moving out there!

Mr. Cool was there, voice easy and under control.

Herky-jerky, right?

Sort'a.

Hold on! The light from the flare makes the shadows jump around. That's what you're seein'.

Ah.

Don't go embarrassing me by shootin' at shadows, All right?

Ok.

Promise?

Yeah.

The action's over there, on the other side of the base for now. They're trying for the ammo dump behind the hill. See?

Yeah.

They don't want us. We're just in the way. Take it easy. Enjoy the show. Wake me up if you need me.

He looked at the M60. Mr. Cool was quiet. He and Dan waited for the fight to come their way. Like Mr. Cool had said, the NVA wanted the ammo dump. The Battalion just happened to be in the way.

The NVA and Marines went at each other in squad-size firefights on the ridgeline between the base and the ammo dump. The fight clawed its way downhill toward the perimeter and the tower. Dan could hear the AKs and the M16s but they were all mixed up. He saw a single muzzle flash, a quick burst of automatic fire, red tracers reaching out, then green going the other way.

Little by little the gun fire stopped as the fighters on the hill ran out of ammo and the fight continued with the knives and the kicking, choking, gouging and biting. When it was over, the surviving Marines somehow ended up with the empty AKs, and the dead and captured NVA had the empty M16s.

Things slowed down and he and Mr. Cool catnapped through what was left of the night. Just before dawn, Dan heard a rumble from offshore.

"Naval gunfire." Said the squad leader. "That'll keep everybody's heads down for a while. You guys can get some sleep."

Dan curled up in a corner of the tower with a sandbag for a pillow. He slept like a baby with the sweet sound of naval gunfire arching overhead like a mother's lullaby.

Chapter Fifteen

The weather was either cooling with the approaching monsoon season, or Dan was finally adapting to the heat and humidity. Steve was gone. He wasn't coming back and he wasn't going to be replaced. Dan knew that he was all that was left of the Civic Action Program and that he would have to somehow navigate it on his own.

He thought about what Smith had said about the deserters and decided to take the long way around so that he would not have to go in the same way every time. Instead of rolling down the hill into the refugee villages, he turned left and drove up the hill through the checkpoint in front of the First Marine Division.

The Marines waved him through with a smile. Dan waved back and rolled through the checkpoint. Circling downhill through the countryside and back toward the coast, he approached a crossroads with a tiny mom and pop gedunk store selling trinkets to the passing Marines. As he neared the intersection, two young women, "boom–boom" girls, stepped out from behind the shanty and lifted up their tops to display their breasts. He was surprised but not attracted by the display. Not only was he married to Lilly, he was well aware that if there were prostitutes, the warlords or criminal gangs would be close by.

Just before the truck passed through the intersection, a much older woman ran from behind the store to join the girls. She copied the "boom-boom" girls, pulling up her blouse and exposing her own breasts. Her mouth was stained dark red, almost black, from the betel nut. Under the influence of the drug, she was laughing and shaming the girls as they tried to move away from her. Wondering about the inspiration for this little drama, Dan rolled on through the quiet, green countryside of rice fields, each tended by its own small shrine.

When he reached Hoa An, he turned off the main road onto a dusty track that led into an open area bordered by a narrow string of poor shanties. He drove slowly so the truck's big tires would raise as little dust as possible. A young boy tending his baby brother asleep in a hammock looked up at him and smiled sweetly.

Ahead, the track narrowed to little more than a trail where it entered the bamboo forest. Dan slowed and let the truck roll to a stop. From the driver's side window he noticed a lady sitting behind a sewing machine in a humble stand covered with a sheet of old roofing tin and bamboo leaves. She smiled at him.

"Chao Ba," He tried the Vietnamese greeting for a married woman.

Her smile broadened and she said something he did not understand. She gestured toward the trail into the bamboo. Pressing his hands together, he thanked her in Vietnamese, "Cam on."

He slipped the clutch. The truck rolled forward. The bamboo closed behind him. Dan felt the village change around him like a giant single-cell organism. It was alive. Every person, every part of the village, seemed to become aware of his presence at the same time. Somehow, they knew he was there.

He understood that the VC came and went. The deserters and the criminal gangs were always a threat. Yet, the village elders continued to make decisions in the best interests of everyone. The Popular Force troop, Ong Bey and a group of four or five boys too young for the draft, kept the peace and patrolled the village at night.

Somehow they managed to hold it together, maintaining a surprising level of normal village life in the face of the constantly shifting dangers of the war pressing in on all sides. Dan hoped that in some way his presence helped.

That night he wrote Lilly,

> *I know you worry about me, especially now that Steve is gone. You may think it doesn't make sense to work by myself in the village away from the base so much of the time.*

It seems strange even to me, but in many ways I feel safer in the village than I do around some of the people on the base. I do understand that if the villagers wanted to do me harm they could have by now. But for whatever the reasons they have not.

They are very curious about me, just as I am about them. At one of the more recent Med-Caps, I told them I was married and showed the women the picture you gave me from our honeymoon.

The women were amazed at your golden skin and blonde curls. They passed the picture around and around, giggling and chattering among themselves. Every so often they would look up at me, giggle and go back to the picture.

It seems like they wanted to ask many questions but were not able to. Now, when they see me, they smile like we have this secret, this knowledge of you, my sweet bride.

This may not make much sense, but I do believe that one of the reasons I feel safe here is because of you and because we are together. Even so far away you keep me safe. I take you with me everywhere I go.

Chapter Sixteen

Standing in company formation for a midmorning inspection, Dan looked down the line of men next to him. He was assigned to Headquarters Company, where most of the guys tried to be reasonably squared away. He was clearly the exception. His boots were caked with mud and his clothes, along with everything else he owned, had been destroyed when his hootch burned down during the Tet. He'd hacked off his shirtsleeves because of the heat and the edges were badly frayed. He had also given up blousing his trousers, which were muddy and stained with rings of sweat. Even the Civic Action badge pinned to his shirt hung at an odd angle.

When the inspection was over, his squad leader came over to him and said, "Look, Dan, you don't have to show up for these things if you don't want to."

That was fine with him. He figured he must have been making the rest of the company look bad. He looked at his mud-caked boots and said, "Sounds good to me."

The Tet Offensive had played havoc with the villages and they were still unsettled. He understood that the people were struggling to recover from the effects of the intense fighting, and he felt it was his responsibility to be back out there as soon as possible.

He found the village elders beside the trail in the shade of the bamboo where they often met during the heat of the day. A rocket had blown a hole in the ground near the graveyard where Dan and the corpsmen had been holding the Med-Caps. The walls of the elementary school had cracked, and they did not feel that it was safe to use. No one talked about the fighting or the war. No one said VC or NVA or talked about the Skyraiders strafing the rice fields. He wondered what it had been like for them surrounded by enemies on all sides, crouching in whatever safe places they could find, trying to protect the tender flesh of their children from the sharp pieces of the hot metal that filled the air.

They invited him to squat with them in the shade. They talked easily among themselves, sharing small jokes with Dan that he didn't understand but still made him laugh. He was aware of how little he really knew about these men. This village was their world. It was constant and peaceful and they seemed content to live well within it. He was curious about them, and they seemed to be curious about him as well.

Dan couldn't understand the words, but he could see they were trying to include him. He asked one of the boys what they were talking about.

"He say road very good thing."

"Road?"

The boy smiled and nodded. The men smiled and nodded. One of the men pointed to the east side of the rice field and then to the west. Everyone nodded in agreement that it would be a good idea. The men poured Dan more tea. He was beginning to understand that they wanted his help building a road.

He wanted to hear more, but a sudden wave of nausea rose up from his stomach and he turned away and threw up on the ground. He felt better for a short while, but the nausea came back, stronger than before. Dan realized it was heat exhaustion and that he had to get back to the base while he could. He stood up and started walking. Putting one foot in front of the other, he started back to the base. For some reason he forgot about the truck. His vision was shutting down from both sides, and it wasn't long before he threw up again, lost control of his bowels and shat his pants. Dan knew he could go into convulsions, pass-out, and not wake up. That could be the end of him. He kept walking.

The next thing he remembered he was stumbling through the main gate, dragging his M16 by the barrel. He took a half a dozen steps, stumbled to a stop and passed out in the shade of a stone wall.

Someone must have found him there because when he came to he was in the sick bay with the corpsmen trying to reduce his core temperature and giving him sips of tepid salt water to help re-balance his blood chemistry. Bobby Burden gave him an orange soda. When they let him go, he staggered to his hootch, fell into his bunk and passed out.

Dan woke up a day later, drank some fluids, and managed to eat a little to bring his strength back. The truck wasn't where it was supposed to be and he realized that he must have left it somewhere. He didn't say anything to anyone about it and no one asked him. As soon as he was able, he hitched a ride with Hunter, who dropped him off close enough so he could walk on in. The truck was where he had left it.

The boys of the Popular Force were guarding it with their M1 carbines. He was relieved at not loosing the battalion's precious vehicle and thanked them profusely. They smiled and bowed, reminding him of attendants at the valet parking.

It was clear to him that the majority of the Seabees and Marines could not distinguish a Popular Force member from a Viet Cong or any other Vietnamese. Given the good guy, bad guy mentality with which the whole war was being conducted, it was not surprising that the Americans saw every

Vietnamese they encountered as the enemy, or at the least a person of an inferior race.

Most of their contacts were with a Vietnamese person who worked on a military base, a prostitute, or a street vendor, and their relationships seemed to be almost universally defined by their roles within the occupation. Thus, the constant low-level atrocities such as the trucker bumping the village elder off his bicycle were seen as normal behaviors or even some sort of entertainment for the occupying troops. Dan understood that these attitudes and behaviors put him at risk when he was alone in the village. More and more, he felt trapped in a sort of slippery, "no man's land" between the two.

He regretted getting sick and having to leave the meeting with the elders. While he assumed they understood, he was disappointed with himself. He knew he had to earn their trust, yet at the same time the gulf between the Americans and the Vietnamese seemed increasingly insurmountable.

When they finally met again, the elders explained that during the rains the rice field flooded for weeks at a time and the two outside hamlets were isolated. The children couldn't walk to school or the women to market. They were also especially vulnerable to infiltration by the VC. They never talked about it in that way and Dan didn't either. Maybe it was to protect him. He didn't know. He did know that it was their village and that his life was in their hands. Maybe a road was a good idea in more ways than one.

But the road project didn't go anywhere because they couldn't do anything without a bulldozer, and the Battalion wasn't about to let him have one for some place out in the middle of nowhere. The villagers hadn't said anything more about it, but Dan could see the disappointment on their faces when he met them on the trail.

Hoping to requisition one of the battalion's bulldozers, he went to see the Chief Petty Officer in charge of the heavy equipment. The Chief was a lifer who was just putting in his time. He was sitting behind his desk, leaning back with his feet up, looking at a magazine with pictures of naked women.

"You wanna what?" He asked Dan leaning forward, his feet hitting the floor. "You want me to give you one of my D8's so you can take it out there in the jungle and lose it?"

"Not exactly," said Dan. He could see this wasn't going very well.

"What are you doing out there anyway?"

"Well, the village has asked us to help them build a road to connect the hamlets."

"Do you have any idea what a D8 costs?"

Dan shook his head. "Nope."

"Listen, if I do let you have a Cat', you'll take it out there somewhere in Gookland and they'll steal the dang thing an' I'll be screwed for life. What do you think the Navy'll do to me if I lost one of their precious bulldozers? I'd be fucked, that's what. My career in this man's Navy would be over. Besides they're all out on jobs right now and I couldn't give you one if I wanted to, which I don't."

Dan had no idea how to respond. The Chief softened a little, leaned back in his chair, picked up his magazine and said, "Maybe you can get one from one of the ARVN (South Vietnamese Army) units."

Dan was discouraged. He figured maybe he had gone about it the wrong way. The next time he saw Smith he asked him about it.

"Yeah, Dan, try givin' 'em a bottle of booze or somethin' next time. Hell, there's some guys who'll cumshaw (trade) for anything they can get their hands on. You'll think of somethin'. Besides, I think all the Cats' are out on jobs right now anyway."

Chapter Seventeen

After a while, Dan began to realize that regardless of the war, life still insisted on stumbling forward. Special Services managed to get their hands on a movie, *The Green Berets*. They set up some sheets of plywood and painted them white to make a screen. It was the first movie in months, and everyone was going to watch it if they possibly could.

Just like in *The Fighting Seabees* from WWII, John Wayne was a larger than life hero. David Jansen played the cynical reporter, who by the end of the movie, would be convinced that somehow all of this made sense. He just had to hang out with "The Duke" and his "Green Berets" long enough.

The problem was, there was a real war going on in earnest. The NVA were going after the Ammo Dump again and we were surrounded. Mortar crews were firing one round after another while at the same time flare ships were lighting up the night sky. Helicopter gunships were circling and firing a steady stream of red tracer rounds into the dark. Closer to the ammo dump, a Quad .50 (four fifty caliber machine guns in a single mount) was tearing up the night.

But nobody was paying any attention to the real war. It didn't seem to matter. "The Duke" was winning the war for us on the plywood screen.

The Marines and Seabees were watching the movie. The Vietnamese children were watching through the wire. Dan stood in the rear, stunned by the overwhelmingly surreal quality of this strange scene with its dual soundtrack of the Duke's war on the screen and the real war outside the wire. No one else seemed to notice.

He walked up to the Command Post bunker. The Officer of the Day was making coffee. One of the lifers was entertaining everyone in the bunker by reading out loud from the pornographic novel, "The Autobiography of a Flea."

He wished he had something better to do but he didn't so he went back down to watch John Wayne save the day. The Vietnamese orphans were still watching the movie from outside the wire. He wondered what they could possibly be thinking.

It was several days before he was able to sit down and write a letter to Lilly. He told her about the movie and the battle.

> *I realize this may sound a little cynical and I know it's un-American to knock 'the Duke,' but it seems strange to me that people think a guy who has never even been close to a real war is some kind of hero. While he was play-acting at Fort Benning Georgia to sell*

*an endless, pointless war, real people
were actually dying face down in the
mud with their blood and skin and
dreams seeping back into the earth,
already starting to smell bad before
the goddamn movie was even over.*

*We haven't had any mail for a while,
and I miss you more than I can say.*

As the days went by, he told Lilly less and less.
He had written her about Do Ti Thuan and her little
sister, but he had not told her about the cruelty of
the truck drivers "bouncing" people into the ditches
with their trucks. His letters to her were becoming
fewer and fewer as he ran out of good things to say.

He was on one side of the planet and Lilly was
on the other. He was beginning to understand why
the guys in Vietnam called the States "The World."
Maybe Vietnam and the United States were part of
the same planet but they sure weren't part of the
same world. Every day it seemed like they were
moving farther and farther apart, and the thought
of his ever making it back home seemed more and
more unimaginable.

Even though he tried every day to somehow
mitigate the war's mindless atrocities by trying to
help the people in the village survive, the world he
knew was giving way beneath him, and there was

nothing he could do about it. He was being dragged feet first into the black, bottomless pit of this war, and he was determined not to take her with him. At the same time, he was desperate to somehow hang onto the only thing in his life that was clean and decent.

He knew that Lilly was his only hope. It occurred to him that if he shared too much, if he did drag her in behind him, it would destroy them both. She was the only certain thing in a world of fear and chaos.

Her love was a silver chord, a lifeline reaching across the sea to where he was being hammered into something flat and brittle. She was his anchor and he swung hard against it with every tide.

Chapter Eighteen

Dan picked one of the little bananas and sat on the steps of his hootch, watching the red sun rising into the smoke and the smells of the war and the heat of the new day. The base gradually shifted to its daytime activities with the sounds of choppers coming and going through the black smoke of burning shitters and the deep rumble of diesels bringing the morning to life.

The fighting had slowed for a while. Dan was supposed to meet the village elders that morning, so he picked up his truck and drove on out to the village. He parked the truck and hiked through the sleepy morning to where the trails crossed at the graveyard.

He was standing at the intersection waiting for the elders, when a DC-6 airliner, with all four engines screaming crashed through the bamboo over his head. Shattering trees and homes, the massive propellers tore people into pieces as it cut through the village like a giant knife.

He never really heard the crash. It was just one long horrible scream that left him mindless. He ran after the plane, believing there must be something he could do to help.

He tripped and fell over the body of one of the village men who had been dismembered by the wing as it careened along the ground. When he stood up he was covered with the warm pieces of flesh from the man's body. His clothes were soaked with warm blood and bodily fluids. At first he didn't know what it was and tried to brush the pieces of the man off his clothing. A few seconds before, this had been a living, breathing person. Now it was just so many pieces of garbage.

The wreckage of the plane had come to rest at the edge of the bamboo. One wing was in the rice field, and the other was at the edge of a clearing where it had scraped the land clean of the bamboo and the houses and the people in them.

The big DC-6 was broken, but for the most part it was still intact. Carrying one hundred and nine Vietnamese dependents, the aviation gas was burning intensely. Some of the passengers had been killed at impact. The rest were trapped alive in the burning plane.

Hearing their screams, he staggered forward, thinking there must be some way he could help, something he could do, but the white-hot flames blew him back, and he just stood there stunned and helpless, covered in blood and gore.

Rescue helicopters from the air base landed in the rice field, and the rescue workers cut into the back of the fuselage with metal-cutting saws. They finally got a woman out. Her clothes had burned off but she was still alive. They carried her on a stretcher to a waiting helicopter. One of the rescuers yelled, "cover her up!" and someone ran up with a blanket for her.

The villagers were watching, wide eyed.

He wandered around in the village until dark and then went back to the base. He tried to dig the clotted ashes and the smell from the burned women and children out of his nose and throat. He got most of the ashes out, but the smell never went away.

The next day he was back in the village. The elders met him at the north end where the road narrowed to a trail as it entered the forest. The woman with the sewing machine was not there. They asked him if he would help them with a burial. He was humbled by their request and felt honored to be included in their private moment. Because the graveyard was on the other side of the village, they would have to go out onto the road, and they asked Dan if he would return in three days to carry the simple wooden casket on the back of his truck.

Dan arrived at their home in the morning on the day of the burial. The person to be buried was the same fellow he had tripped over the day the DC6 had crashed into the village. His family had picked up the pieces and taken him to their home on the other side of the rice field. They had mourned him for three days and now were taking him back to the graveyard to be buried.

The smell of decay and incense were strong in the air. The man's family carried the simple wooden casket from its place of mourning in their humble home and gently lifted him onto the flatbed International. Dan drove slowly down the dirt pathway following the man's family. Not wanting to press them he stopped the truck and waited for them to move ahead.

On each side of the trail the villagers were dropping small pieces of paper with a swatch of silver or gold painted on them. He asked one of the men what they were for.

The man looked at Dan and said gently, "So he can find his way home."

Dan asked, "Is it okay it I have one?"

The man bowed. "Of course."

Dan looked at the little square of paper with it's swatch of silver paint for a long time, trying to understand. Something caught his attention. Looking up, he saw the spirit of the man who had died hurrying back down the trail and past him with a big smile.

He edged the truck carefully out on to the shoulder of the road and slowly crossed the north end of the rice field. Once the procession was past the field he turned back into the shade of the bamboo. He drove past where the plane had crashed, and finally stopped at the graveyard.

The big plane had just fallen out of the sky, and no matter how he tried, he could not make sense of it. It had been so close. A few feet lower and someone would have been picking up the pieces of what was left of him.

He watched as the last shovel full of dirt was placed over the grave. Then the men with the shovels in their hands, turned back into their day's work in the fields of rice. He looked at the silver paper in his hand and remembered the man on the trail saying, "So he can find his way back home."

It had seemed so dignified and so safe. There wasn't any talk that he was in "a better place" or a need to "celebrate his life." It was very simple. He had just come home to stay in a place where he was loved. Dan wondered if that was part of what the elders had told him when they had said "Each home is a shrine."

Chapter Nineteen

The next time Dan was at the Bo De School, Ong De advised him that the high school students were planning their "Ditch Day" and asked him to help take them to the beach at Namo.

"Ditch Day?" Dan asked.

Ong De smiled at him. "They wish to go to the beach at Namo."

"Namo?" He didn't like the sound of it. Dan knew Namo was one of the places where the Viet Cong set up and fired their rockets at the ammo dump. But that's where they wanted to go, so in spite of his misgivings, he said, "Ok, I'll see what I can do."

He had no idea how he would do it, but he couldn't turn them down. He went to the XO. The XO was second in command and one of the crusty old-style officers who looked like he might bite your head off.

But he had bought a scholarship for one of the students at the school and had even gone down for the presentation. Dan remembered how the craggy-faced gentleman had left his seat and knelt on one knee to the level of the child and how the little boy had bowed so sweetly and so sincerely. And how each one, the man and the child, had held onto their end of the award, neither one wanting to let go of that moment.

"Ditch Day?" The XO chuckled. "I thought that was a custom of American teenagers."

Dan shrugged and raised his hands helplessly. "It beats me Sir. I don't know what to tell you. That's what they want to do."

"I think we can dig up a couple of transport vehicles. The guys call them "cattle cars.""

"Thank you Sir."

The XO smiled and chuckled to himself.

When the day finally came, they filled both of the transporters with scrubbed and excited students in their best clothes. The rest crowded into the back of his dump truck, and they took off for the beach at Namo.

When they arrived at Namo, the students and teachers went to the beach, and the drivers returned to base with the transporters. Dan was aware that Namo was a location where the enemy often fired rockets at the air base and ammo dump, and the few buildings still intact were scared with bullet holes.

However, it was also a beach resort favored by the local Vietnamese for its fine white beach and decent restaurant that sat out in the bay on an island connected to the beach by a bridge. Perhaps more to the point, it was also off limits to American servicemen. He stashed his forty-five under the seat of the truck and locked the doors. This seemed like a really bad idea, but he couldn't take it swimming.

Ong De asked Dan to join him, and they swam out to the restaurant through the warm water, racing each other, then laughing at the fun of it. They dried off on the patio, where Ong De bought Dan a non-alcoholic coconut cocktail that was a delicacy to him and a mystery to Dan. They talked about the students, the school, and the wonder of a world with both east and west, and how they could be so different in so many ways.

For example, Dan suggested, "Like the time the dentist tried to teach Chaplain Hu to play checkers?"

Ong De nodded, and they both laughed, remembering how the dentist had brought a set of checkers with him to the school with the intention of teaching Chaplain Hu how to play the game.

Although Chaplain Hu was a Buddhist priest, there was nothing meek or mild about him. He was absolutely fearless and had little tolerance for fools, especially those who looked down their nose at him. After politely following the Dentist's instructions for playing checkers, he had signaled to one of the teachers who was watching nearby. The teacher left and returned with a magnificent, hand-carved ivory chess set.

While the ornate chessboard was similar to checkers or chess, the intricately carved ivory pieces were altogether different. There were mandarins, lumbering elephants, tigers, and massive cannon on an equally massive chessboard. It was unlike anything Dan had ever imagined.

Not only were the pieces and their moves completely different, the atmosphere resembled a cockfight more than a quiet game of chess. An excited group of fifteen or twenty students and teachers stood behind each player, yelling encouragement, commenting, laughing and offering instructions to the Dentist on one side and Chaplain Hu on the other. Of course, it was all in Vietnamese, so it did the Dentist no good whatsoever.

After the game had gone on for a while, Chaplain Hu lifted one of the artillery pieces over his head, and with a loud "kiai", slammed it down on the other side of the board. To everyone's delight, chess pieces flew in every direction and the game was over.

When they were done remembering, Ong De looked across the table at Dan and said, "You seem troubled."

"The plane crash in the village."

Ong De nodded.

"It came down right over my head. I could have almost reached out and touched it."

Ong De said, "They came to see their loved ones, their sons and husbands and sweethearts in the Vietnamese army at Da Nang. It was a great day for them."

"That ended so badly."

"Yes, and you were there to witness it."

"I heard their cries for help, I smelled their burning flesh, Ong De, and I could not help them."

His teacher took a sip of the coconut cocktail and looked out across the water to the horizon of the South China Sea. They were silent with their thoughts, all the loose ends, all the unanswerable questions swirling in the air above their heads like the souls of those who perished in the crash of the airplane.

Ong De said, "There are some things we cannot help, or even comprehend. Maybe the understanding will come to us in time. Maybe it never will. Either way, we recognize that this terrible event is also part of the whole and that like all things, it will be brought into balance."

Dan didn't understand. "I don't get it."

Ong De smiled at him. "Sometimes we must accept what is, so we can prepare for what is coming next."

Dan looked at him.

Ong De said, "Okay, let me put it this way. If I'm shaking my fist and cursing the truck that just now splashed mud on my trousers, I may not see the one that will soon run me over."

Chapter Twenty

An Phong was the oldest boy in a group of orphans. They had no place to live and did not attend school. They worked at anything they could find and at night they slept in the "no man's land" between the Marines and the village of Phouc Thoung.

As the oldest, An Phong accepted the responsibility for their safety and welfare. He did his best to provide what he could by selling "gedunk," imitation combat ribbons and other black-market trinkets, to the Marines and Seabees on the road. Like part of the landscape, An Phong and the other orphans were always around, but they never seemed to create any problems for anyone.

However, most of the guys saw them as a nuisance, or worse, as a vague sort of threat, just because they were Vietnamese. It was kind of like the whole war. Some of the guys would try to help the people, but it seemed like most just saw them as the enemy.

Regardless of how he was treated, Phong always had a dignified manner and a big smile for everyone.

One day, hoping to make a sale, he approached the Marine checkpoint and was told to stay away. He returned a couple of days later and the guard shot him in the leg, breaking the bone. The battalion's corpsmen picked him up and took him to the sick bay where they set his leg in a cast, and fitted him with crutches.

Undaunted, he still came every day. He hobbled around on his crutches, offering his gedunk to anyone who would buy it. Because he had already been shot, it seemed like no one felt like shooting him again.

A few nights later, Special Services nailed up some plywood, painted it white and showed a movie. The Seabees and Marines were sitting on anything they could find, watching *Sweet November* with Sandy Dennis and Anthony Newley. Other than the *Green Berets* it was the only movie they had seen in months. Phong and the other children were watching it through the concertina wire that defined the boundary between the village and the base. Some of the guys didn't like it. It was "their movie," and they were not inclined to share it with "no gooks."

The men were all armed and had been drinking heavily. After grumbling about the "gooks" watching their movie, one of the men stood up and threw a rock the size of a baseball at them. It was a long, hard throw, and it hit Phong directly on his broken leg, shattering the cast and once again breaking the bone.

Dan heard Phong cry out and could see the boy writhing on the ground in pain. The other children were shocked and scared. Dan was shocked, but not surprised. The men went back to watching the movie.

From where Dan was standing in the back, it wasn't far to the front gate, and without thinking, he went outside the wire to get him. Once he picked Phong up, he realized that he had to get him to the sick bay that was a couple hundred yards up the hill. Phong was in pain, but after the shock of getting hit he didn't cry out or complain.

Even though Phong was just a teenager, he was big for a Vietnamese, and because of his pain, he was dead weight. He could carry Phong half way around the base to the side gate, which may or may not, be open. Or he could carry him through the crowd, between the men and their movie, straight back up the hill to the sick bay.

He looked at the men to see if there was anyone he knew who could give him a hand. He didn't see any friendly faces. All the men were watching the movie intently, their green uniform backs closing ranks to protect their own.

Unwilling to abandon Phong in pain, Dan carried him up the trail between the projector and the screen, between the men and their movie, casting larger-than-life silhouettes on the screen.

He left Phong with the Corpsmen and went down to the command bunker. The officer in charge was his Company Commander, Lt. McConnell. McConnell was one of the good guys. Dan liked him and hated to cause him trouble, but he reported the incident to him and asked him to arrest the rock-thrower. Dan could tell he wasn't too excited about it.

"We gotta do something," Dan said, his head down like he was studying the floor for an answer.

McConnell looked at him and said, "I'm not going down there alone."

They looked at each other for a while. Dan hated to put him on the spot like that, but he was disgusted and pissed off and was about to do something stupid like pulling the plug or knocking over the projector, anything, just to make sure this brutality was not ignored. The Lieutenant could see Dan was starting to come unwound. Looking carefully at him, he said, "You're coming with me, right?"

Dan nodded in the affirmative.

He understood why the Lieutenant had hesitated and he didn't blame him. He was apprehensive and so was Dan. Anyone with good sense would be. The men had been drinking beer for several hours. They were all carrying M16s, and M1 carbines, and they had made it pretty clear what they thought about the "gooks" watching their movie. Dan hadn't planned on spending his evening this way, but he was in too deep to back out now.

So he and Lt. McConnell went down the hill. The men were trying to watch the only movie they had seen in months. They were holding their weapons tight, their drunken disdain like a banner, one eye on the movie and the other on Dan and the Lieutenant.

Dan led the Lieutenant through the rows of unyielding, pissed off Seabees and Marines to where the man who had thrown the rock was sitting surrounded by his like-minded buddies.

Dan pointed to the man he wanted arrested and stood back. Lt. McConnell motioned for the guy to come with him. He sat there for a minute, looking up at the Lieutenant knowing he had done wrong, but not wanting to admit it in front of his friends. Finally, he handed his M16 to the man next to him and came along like the good soldier he probably was most of the time.

They escorted him up the hill to the command bunker. Dan left him with Lieutenant McConnell and went back to the sick bay to check on Phong. The Corpsmen had given him an orange soda and were fixing him up with a new cast. Phong gave Dan a big smile and saluted him with the bottle of soda.

He had started a letter to Lilly earlier that night, and it was waiting for him when he got back to his hootch.

> *I feel like I'm caught between two worlds that never will understand each other. We don't have any desire to understand the Vietnamese in the surrounding villages, and the Americans' actions are incomprehensible to the villagers. Even when it seems like there might be some sort of understanding, it usually turns out I was wrong. The problem for me is that I always seem to be in the middle.*

Smith caught up with him a few days later. "Still livin' dangerously, huh Dan?"

"What do you mean?"

"Arresting that guy during the movie."

Dan thought about it. "Yeah. Maybe it wasn't the smartest thing to do." He shrugged, "It was a fucked up thing to do to that kid. "

"Well, you made your point, but you're sure not makin' many friends."

"Why would I want to be friends with a guy like that?"

Smith looked at him and grinned, "What about me?"

Dan laughed, "You're one of a kind, Smith."

Smith raised his eyebrows as if to say, *look who's calling the kettle black.*

Shaking his head, Smith went on. "Some of the guys on the shit detail are calling you White Cong."

Dan said, "I know, Durwood and the shit detail, but I can't worry about it or I'd never get out of bed, much less go back into the village."

"Just watch your step, Dan." He picked up his M16. "I can't help ya' out there."

Smith knew how it worked. Dan offered him a Pall Mall. "No thanks, gotta go."

"See ya," said Dan, "And thanks." Smith looked back over his shoulder and gave him a quick salute.

As he lit the Pall Mall, Dan remembered an old Marine at the bus station in Oxnard. Waiting for the next shuttle bus to the base he had dropped his sea bag and taken a seat in the lobby when he heard someone say, "You ain't seen shit."

An old man leaned forward from his seat across the room. He sat in the middle of three dirty plastic chairs wedged between the quarter lockers and the free publications. His worn field jacket was covered with combat medals from past and distant wars.

He said it again, "You ain't seen shit."

Time and wine had left him overcooked and hard-wrinkled. "Got a smoke for an ol' soger?" It was less a question than a tired chant.

Dan shook his head. "Don't smoke."

The man in the chair looked at him and said in a calm, quiet voice just loud enough for Dan to hear, "You will."

The old vet looked across the room at two soldiers waiting for their bus and raised his ragged voice. "Anyone got a smoke for an ol' Marine?"

Squirming under his unforgiving eyes that had seen too much, they tried to ignore him and turned away, laughing to themselves.

He cursed them for their callow smugness. "I was at Guadalcanal. I...was there...I was. Anyone got a smoke for a marine?"

He was yelling now, turning to the whole room where people were being careful to pretend he did not exist at all. "I was a marine... I was there... you bunch of no good..."

His voice trailed off as his head dropped into his hands.

Thump, thump, thump, ta thump, a young boy dribbled his basketball through the door of the depot, pushing it open without missing a beat and past the old soldier. Pretending it was the last second of the playoffs for the championship of the universe, he feinted a pass to the Pepsi machine and bounced the ball off the top row of lockers to score the winning point. Then without stopping he dribbled on into the restroom, thump, a-de-thump, thump.

Between his fingers the old man mumbled, "The war...you don't...how 'bout a smoke?" No one was listening. Dan sat watching the used up old soldier. He raised his head and looked at Dan, unexpectedly clear-eyed and terribly sane. He said, "I was like you once."

Dan held his gaze, nodded, beginning to understand. The man repeated, "I was."

The door to the restroom opened with a thump-a-de-thump. Basketball boy faked it casually past the swinging door, dribbled down the center of the dirty room and out into the hard daylight of the street.

The shuttle bus pulled in and stopped just outside the door. Dan stood up, crossed the room, and took the old Marine's hard, blooded hands in his own.

The old vet clutched Dan's hands, looked him in the eye and said, "I was like you once."

"I believe you." Dan said, "I believe you."

Now he remembered that the old Maine had asked him for a cigarette and he had said he didn't smoke and the Vet had said, "You will," and now he was.

He also remembered him saying, "You ain't seen nothin'."

Well, he had seen some things he hadn't expected. Every day was something new. At the same time he had a pretty good idea there was more to come.

Chapter Twenty-One

It was a lazy mid-morning. Dan had enjoyed a late breakfast with his friend Michael Peacock, who was the Battalion Photographer's Mate. They had been talking about their parents and wondering what it must be like for them to have a son in Vietnam.

It made Dan think how long it had been since he had written his mother and father, and he was on his way back to the hootch to write them a letter. He had one foot on the bottom step to his hootch when a thin, elderly Vietnamese man ran frantically downhill between the hootches, plastic sandals flapping on his bony feet. Little more than a skeleton in worn white pants and shirt with short-cropped white hair, the elder ran by Dan wailing out loud and waving his hands in the air.

Dan wasn't used to seeing a Vietnamese cry but the old man's hands and pants were covered with feces. Durwood was chasing him with a bamboo stick.

Durwood saw Dan and stopped. His face was red and twitchy, his lips pulled back from his teeth. He spat when he tried to talk.

Shaking the stick, he yelled at Dan, "Where's that son of a bitch? Where is he?"

Dan held up his hands and asked, "What's going on Durwood?"

"That papa-san won't do his job. He won't do what I tell him."

"So you're gonna beat him with that stick?"

Durwood spat at Dan's feet. "Damn right. Out of my way, gook lover."

Dan stepped toward him, looked him in the eye and said, "I'm not in your way, mulefucker."

Durwood went white, raised his arm like he was going to strike him. Instead he yelled, "You son of a bitch, gook-lovin' bastard. You'll get yours!" Then he turned and stumbled back up the hill, beating the bamboo stick on the side of each hootch he passed.

A Vietnamese lady who worked on the base had joined Dan and was standing quietly by his side. Ba Wi and Dan had crossed paths enough to say hello. He could tell she was pissed.

"Woodad numba ten! He throw papa-san in shit can. Papa-san not do this work. Not pick up shit! Not proper for papa-san. Not proper for grandfather! Grandfather numba one. Woodad numba ten!"

She looked to see if Dan understood her. He did.

"Woodad hit grandpa with stick, push grandpa in shit can! He no good, no goddamn good numba ten GI!"

Dan shook his head. What could he do? The military toilets on most of the bases in Vietnam were basic outhouses. The bottom one-quarter of a fifty-gallon steel drum was placed under the seat to catch the waste. There was a flap in the back of the shitter and once a day the cans were pulled out, filled with diesel fuel and the waste was burned. Hence the beautiful red sunrises over the South China Sea.

Naturally, no one wanted the job, and there was no way that someone like Durwood could imagine that, unlike in the States, elders were revered almost as deities in Vietnam and were never demeaned or shamed in any way.

Dan shook his head and looked at Ba Wi. He could see she was angry. Durwood was gone. The old man was gone. Ba Wi looked at him, shook her head in disgust and walked away.

He knew she was right. Except for today she had never failed to greet him with a broad smile, and "Choa An", as a young man, or son. He would greet her in turn with "Choa Ba", the formal Vietnamese greeting appropriate to an older, or married woman.

On one occasion she had stopped and pointed to the Civic Action badge pinned to his shirt pocket that was written in Vietnamese.

"Yan Su Vu." She had said, smiling broadly.

He nodded and said, "Da" (yes).

She nodded, "Yan Su Vu numba one. Bacshi (doctor) numba one. You bring Bacshi, Hoa An.

"You live Hoa An?" He asked.

She shook her head. She said she lived somewhere but Dan couldn't make out where. She continued saying, "Baschi numba one. Yan Su Vu numba one."

"Cam on." He watched her walk away through the stronghold of the occupying army with the confidence and serene grace of a woman secure in herself and of her place in the world.

Chapter Twenty-Two

Dan had just sat down on the steps of his hootch when the ammunition dump on the other side of the hill erupted into a massive fireball. With the force of a nuclear bomb, the shock wave flew across the earth, smashing everything in its path. Rolling down the hill like an invisible tsunami, it picked Dan up and threw him against what was left of his hootch.

He stayed on the ground, watching the black mushroom cloud tower up and over him, blotting out the sun and then each little corner of blue sky. He didn't know what day it was or what he had been doing before the blast. He was too stunned to wonder what had happened and just lay there watching the day suddenly become night, wondering if it would last forever.

Still watching the sky, he crawled to the mortar trench and fell in head first as the concussion of the next blast filled the air with debris and hammered him against the side of the trench. His friend Michael Peacock dove into the other end and said, "What the hell?"

"Look at the sky!" said Dan.

"What the hell?"

It blew again, driving the air out of his lungs and pounding him into the dirt. There was nothing else.

The rest of the world ceased to be. Dan crouched in the trench, shaking from the last blast, sore in his bones. He clenched into a tight ball, waiting for the next blast never knowing when it would pick up the earth and shake it.

Two more guys tumbled into the other end of the trench. About thirty feet long and four feet deep, the trench was covered with steel plates, with sand bags on top.

The explosions came with no pattern or warning. Full pallets of five hundred and one thousand pound bombs exploded together in one giant blast. The earth split and gave way. The steel sagged under the weight of the sand bags piled above, forcing Dan and the others to the far end of the trench.

Between explosions, they watched the black mushroom clouds that towered over them like sudden mountains, scattering debris and unexploded munitions across the countryside. A one-five-five artillery round landed in the trench next to them, unexploded, nose in the dirt. They moved away from it, inching toward the other end of the trench, trying to keep someone else between the round and their suddenly tender flesh. The base was gone, blown flat, the wreckage from the buildings spread over the burning hillside.

Even though the earth was splitting and the sky was falling all around them, certain acts of nature were still necessary, so they designated one end of the trench for a toilet.

"I have to go, bad," said Peacock.

Dan pointed at the end of the trench. Michael was Dan's best friend in the Battalion. He was the Battalion photographer and a true southern gentleman in every way. He had gone into the village several times with Dan, taking pictures that he generously developed and shared.

"I can't go here," he said.

There was a "four holer" about fifty feet up the hill, and so far it was one of the only buildings still standing.

Michael said, "I'm going up there."

"Come on, Michael. Don't do that."

"It's been quiet for a while. It'll be okay. I really have to go."

"Use the trench, man. We'll look the other way."

"I can't do it."

"Mike please!"

But he was gone, jumping out of the trench and running up the hill to the four-holer. Everyone watched him dash up the hill and duck into the little building. He had only been inside about twenty seconds when there was another massive explosion. The concussion knocked the shitter flat, blew the wreckage down the hill, and left Michael sitting on the toilet, pants down around his ankles, untouched.

He came running down the hill, pulling up his pants, jumped into the trench and said, "Oh no! I forgot to wipe!"

Night came and the eruptions continued without warning, sometimes quiet for a while, then tearing the sky into big chunks of red lightening under the billowing smoke. They hadn't had anything to eat or drink, and Dan could feel the effects of the heat exhaustion coming on. Time was only measured by the interval between the last eruption and the next. Dan crept to the other end of the trench to keep from being buried alive as the cracks in the earth widened, and the top of the trench sagged under the weight of the sand bags piled on top of it. He threw up what little bile there was left in his stomach and passed out.

It was dark and the rats came out. Drawn by the bile, they ran across his chest then went for his eyes, their whiskers brushing his face. He came to all at once, spitting, cursing, and waving his arms, brushing the rats away from his eyes and face. Everyone else had gone, and he knew he didn't want to stay there any longer.

Bobby Burden crawled over with a little cup of orange juice.

"What happened?" Asked Dan.

"Someone said the Marines were burning back some weeds and the ammo dump caught fire."

"You're kidding."

"That's the story."

The massive blasts were fewer and fewer. Dan crawled out of the trench and stumbled over to what was left of the sick bay and sat against the rubble waiting for the morning.

The sky was clearing, and parts of the base, including his hootch, were still burning. Looking across the wreckage, Dan could see an almost limitless supply of scrap lumber and bent roofing tin that could be used to rebuild the village. The lumber was broken and full of nails and the tin was often bent out of shape, but in this part of the world it was priceless.

The Seabees began clearing the mangled buildings and debris with front-end loaders and big diesel dump trucks. The truck drivers were hauling what they saw as scrap to the commercial dumps. Dan's time in the villages had left him with a reasonable certainty that those dumps were extremely valuable 'gold mines' with the immense profits going to the warlords and eventually the VC.

He also saw some of the drivers cruising the villages in an effort to trade their load of scrap lumber and roofing tin for sex or whatever else they could wrangle in trade from the desperate villagers.

One of the truck drivers who had bought a scholarship at the Bo De School drove back through the gate for another load.

Dan waved him down and jumped up on the running board,

"Hey Rick, this stuff going to the commercial dumps?"

"Yeah."

"Isn't that kind of a bad idea?"

The driver shrugged,

"It's not up to me. I just take it where I'm told."

"Who said?"

"This is a huge mess we got here and they want it cleaned up as soon as possible."

"Who told you where to go?"

"Guys are going different places..."

"Who told you to take this stuff to the dump?"

Rick looked around the yard and back at Dan like he wished he would leave him alone.

"Where else would we take it?"

"Whose orders?"

"Senior Chief. He seems to be the man with the plan around here."

Dan nodded but didn't get off the running board. Rick said, "Look, I gotta do what I'm told, right?"

"Right, thanks."

Dan jumped down and the truck rolled on up the hill. He watched another truck, stuffed with enough debris to make someone rich, roll on out through the gate.

Dan pulled out his K-Bar and tested the edge with his thumb. Good enough. He shoved it back in its sheath and went looking for the Senior Chief. The empty trucks returned through the side gate, loaded and left out the front. The Senior Chief's office by the main gate was locked up.

Dan went to the command bunker but the Senior Chief wasn't around. The OD was new and seemed to think the base had been attacked. Dan left the bunker and went to find Lt. McConnell. No luck.

He gave up and walked to his truck, fired it up and backed up to a pile of relatively decent plywood. He was loading the plywood onto his truck, sheet by sheet, when the Chaplain found him and started to help.

"Where you taking this stuff?"

"Out to the village. The concussion from the ammo dump destroyed the elementary school."

The Chaplain lifted one side of a sheet of plywood, shook the dirt off it and tossed it on the truck. An empty six-by rolled in the back gate for another load. They watched it roll by, the big tires trailing dust. They kept loading, talking while they worked. The Chaplain was good help. He paused and asked, "Will any of this help the people out there?"

Dan grabbed another sheet, rolled it over and tossed it on the back of the truck. "Their places got knocked down just like ours. They are in bad shape. I'm taking what I can out to Hoa An. Their elementary school was damaged to the point where it is unsafe and they can't use it."

Dan stopped and waved his hand at the flattened hootches. He was sweating and weak from the heat. "I have to tell you. What we call 'trash' is worth more than we can imagine. Out there 'wood is gold.' Someone's getting very rich off this mess. The dumps are run by the warlords and criminal gangs. The VC are making out on this and the Senior Chief is telling these guys to dump it in their laps while the people in the villages are in worse shape every day."

Dan paused and wiped the sweat out of his eyes. The Chaplain was sweating through his shirt. He said, "I'll see what I can do."

Dan loaded on some of the better roofing tin and took the back way out to Hoa An.

When he got back, Rick stopped his Six-by and stuck his head out the window and yelled at Dan.

"They tell me we're supposed to dump this stuff in the 'ville. That right?"

Dan was impressed. The Chaplain hadn't wasted any time. The trucks were already dumping in the parts of the villages that had been the most damaged.

One of the returning drivers pulled up to where Dan was standing and started yelling at him.

"As soon as we stopped, hell, even before we stopped they were all over the truck, stripping it! I couldn't dump anything without hitting someone! I can't do this, man. I'm goin' to the dump."

A couple more drivers pulled up and jumped out of their trucks, diesel motors rumbling, and started yelling at him. "This is crazy! We can't do this!

Dan knew it was dangerous for them and the villagers, but he also knew they were pissed off because they were losing out on the easy money, sex and whatever else they were getting for a load of 'trash'. He asked the drivers. "Can you dump without stopping the truck?"

"What'd ya mean?" It was a chorus.

"Just slow down as much as you can and dump the load while the truck is moving."

"Yeah. We can do that but what's gonna happen then?"

"Who knows? Maybe you can string out the load so everyone can have a shot at it. It might keep them off the trucks."

They weren't impressed. "Hope you're right."

He said, "Let's give it a try. The people out there don't have food or water or a place to live. We might as well give 'em what we can."

The truckers left shaking their heads. Dan knew they didn't like it, but they knew he was serious and would turn them in if they tried to free-lance it. He knew they resented him for interfering, but at the same time he could see them rising to meet the challenge of doing an impossible job well.

He went to his truck and began sorting out some of the better lumber and roofing tin for another trip to Hoa An.

An empty truck pulled up and stopped, diesel engine rumbling. The Senior Chief was looking at him from the passenger side window. Dan surmised that this was the Senior Chief's big score and he was getting in the way.

The Senior Chief spoke quietly, his scrawny neck, beady eyes and thin reptilian lips twisted into an ugly, menacing sneer. He pointed at Dan out the window and said, "Gook lover. Fuck you, you fucking gook lover."

The driver looked around the Senior Chief, "Hey, White Cong!"

He was pointing his finger at Dan like it was a gun, yelling, "We shoot White Cong!"

The Senior Chief nodded and grinned. The driver jammed the big dump into gear and left, spewing black smoke from the stack. While most of the drivers would do the right thing, the Senior Chief's cronies would do as they pleased, regardless.

Dan had no time to worry about it. He had a job to do. He went back to loading his truck with the broken plywood and bent roofing tin for the village.

White Cong, huh? White Cong were fair game. Fair game to be shot on sight. In their sick, twisted minds, the Senior Chief and his gang of perverts believed they had cause. All they needed was the opportunity, and in this chaos they had plenty of opportunity.

He finished loading the truck and stacked the better pieces of plywood and roofing tin for the next load.

He was on his way to the village when he had to slow at the intersection. He could see the truck drivers following their orders, dumping without stopping, keeping up their speed and spreading the loads in a long line beside the road where the villagers could take it for themselves. It was working like he had hoped. Even so, he could see just how desperate the villagers were.

He watched a Vietnamese man jump on the back of one of the big dumps and climb to the top of the stack of broken lumber and bent steel. The truck was moving fast, and the dump bed rose higher and higher into the air.

The load of broken boards, wood with nails and bent roofing tin was stuck in the bed and wouldn't move. As the bed rose, the man grabbed pieces of wood and threw them to his wife and children as they ran alongside, trying to keep up with the truck. Finally, as the bed extended all the way to almost vertical, the load let go all at once. The man went down with it disappearing into a cloud of dust.

Dan couldn't see him after that. He turned left at the intersection and sped toward Hoa An, determined to deliver his load into the hands of the village elders at the damaged elementary school.

He drove in the back way to the village looking for the seamstress. She wasn't there. He passed her empty stand and entered the bamboo forest looking for a friendly face. There was no one around. He took it slow, keeping the dust and the noise down, grateful he was driving the gas-powered bobtail.

The trail opened into a small clearing where the damaged schoolhouse set to one side in the shade of the bamboo.

The villagers were gathered around the little school looking at the cracks in the unreinforced concrete walls. It was unsafe. They unloaded the wood and roofing tin while the elders were showing him the damage to the school.

They brought the tea and shared their concern at the loss of the school and their hope that came with the new materials he had brought them. They were already making plans for a new, larger, two-room school. Squatting together, they drank the tea, sketching out the plans in the dirt for him to see. It had taken him months to be able to squat for hours at a time, but now it was as natural to him as sitting in a chair.

He was just saying his goodbyes when a big six-by dieseled down the trail and stopped. The driver got out, saw Dan, and knew he was busted. The truck was full of trash.

"I'm looking for the dump."

Dan looked at the villagers. They were silent, looking straight ahead. He knew the driver was looking for something, but it wasn't the dump.

"You're in the wrong place."

"Okay, okay."

He got back in the truck and asked, "Do you know where the dump is?"

"Yeah. So do you."

Dan waved him out, but the villagers motioned they wanted the driver to go ahead and dump the load there. Dan pointed at the load. "Trash, it's trash. Numba Ten."

They motioned with their hands for the driver to dump.

Dan hollered at the driver to wait.

The discussion with the villagers went on. There was no interpreter and his Vietnamese always seemed to fail him when he needed it most. He pointed at the load.

"Numba Ten, no good Hoa An."

Now there were more villagers nodding and smiling and motioning for the driver to dump. He gave in and said to the driver. "Ok, go ahead and dump it."

The driver was happy to oblige and get out of there. The truckload of trash slid out onto the ground in front of the damaged school. Dan shook his head and stepped back while the villagers moved in. Within five minutes the ground was picked clean. Dan stood, stunned. They had found a use, some value, in every bit of what the Americans, himself included, had thought was nothing more than trash.

He was surprised by how little he still knew about them. He had been in the village almost every day for the best part of a year and the differences continued to scramble what he thought was reality.

He remembered reading field studies of Amazon tribes in his Anthropology classes and how the authors, in the comfort of their methodologies, had been so certain, so comfortable with their findings.

Lilly, she had been so far away for so long. He had changed for sure. What was the craziness of this war doing to her? They had run out of things to write in a letter a long time ago but her letters still came every day. He knew she sat down at least once a day and thought of him.

Chapter Twenty-Three

The Seabees were doing what Seabees do best, and Dan was surprised at the rate the buildings on base were being repaired and rebuilt. The villagers seemed to be pleased with the new schools that had been financed by the sudden wealth of the scrap lumber and the Med-Caps had settled into a regular rhythm.

Once a week, sometime around mid-morning, Dan and Bobby Burden and the Chief Corpsman would drive either the stake bed or the bob-tail dump to the intersection where the trails came together near the graveyard. Unlike their first experience, the Med-Caps here were quiet and orderly, with everyone having a chance to be seen and treated.

He was amazed at the Corpsmen's competence and gentleness with the people, carefully diagnosing and treating each person before they moved on to the next.

After his game of "checkers" had gone so wrong, the Dentist had decided not to return to the village, so Thompson, a Dental Technician, set up a workspace off the back of Dan's truck where he took "referrals" from the Corpsmen. Thompson was tall and gangly with a shaggy head of dark hair. He never wore a cap and he looked like he would be more at home changing truck tires than performing oral surgery.

But Dan could see that whatever social graces he might have lacked, were more than compensated for by his skill, enthusiasm, and good humor.

Thompson soon established a "practice" among the many women who suffered from chronic toothache as a result of sacrificing the limited calcium in their diets during pregnancy and childbirth. With no dental care of any kind, many women were forced to chew betel nut to ease the pain. A powerful narcotic, it turned their mouths dark red, almost black. It also created feelings of euphoria and disassociation that played havoc with the relationships within their family and community.

Thompson's first patient was terrified by the oversized stainless steel needle used to administer the local anesthetic. He pulled the needle back and teased her by pretending to accidentally give the shot to himself. He rolled his eyes and clowned, chattering to her in gibberish until she relented, closed her eyes and opened her mouth. The Novocain took the edge off the pain of the toothache and she was able to relax. Thompson quickly removed the offending tooth, holding it up in his pliers for everyone to see. A cheer went up from the other women and his patient stood up, smiling at the miracle. Touching her jaw in amazement she thanked Thompson and proudly walked past the line of women now waiting their turn.

Thompson's "practice" of loyal women soon expanded as the women brought their friends to each Med-Cap. They watched him work his magic, oohing and aahing and touching their jaws.

As they returned each week, Dan could see some of their youth and beauty and sanity being restored to them. Their mouths were no longer stained red and their faces were no longer distorted by the pain and the madness of the betel nut.

He was at his usual station dispensing worm medicine to a long line of children with distended stomachs, when two marines walked into the clearing. One was a tall, slender black guy with a big smile and the other was a shorter white guy with dark, bushy hair and a mustache. Both of them were smiling.

Dan was surprised and thrilled to see them. He waved and jumped down from the truck. "Hey guys, welcome!"

The black guy grabbed his hand. They stood there holding hands and grinning at each other. "I'm Ty, this here's Ragatz, the Sarge."

Ragatz stepped forward and shook hands. Dan introduced the Corpsmen who said "Hi" and went back to their work.

Ty said, "Hey Sarge, it's the Civic Action Seabee!"

Ragatz grinned, "Yeah, we've heard about ya down here. We've been assigned to Civic Action just north of here."

"Whereabouts?"

"As near as we can tell somewhere between Hoa An and Hoa Binh."

"Shit, we're neighbors!" Dan wanted to hug them both.

Ragatz said, "Come up and check us out."

"I will, first chance I get."

They waved and walked back the way they had come. Ty turned and waved. Dan waved until they disappeared into the bamboo.

Seeing the two Marines made him realize how lonely he had become. The next time he had an opportunity he hiked up to their camp. He wasn't sure where it was but knew the general direction. Their cigarette smoke through the bamboo led him the rest of the way.

He remembered the drill instructors teaching them how to "field strip" a cigarette so the enemy wouldn't know where they were. He wondered why no one seemed to be concerned about the smell of the smoke from their C-ration cigarettes? Hell, it was like bacon in the forest. He couldn't miss it.

Ty greeted him with a big smile, dancing around with his long black arms open wide like he was going to give Dan a big hug. He laughed and said, "Here comes the Seabee! We just got some new C-rats', Dan, Pork and Beans!

"I think I'll stick to the spaghetti," said Dan. "Where's Ragatz?"

"Back in the bushes doin' his business. Here he comes."

Dark bushy hair, big mustache, no hat, green USMC towel around his neck, big smile.

"Hey Dan."

"How are ya, Sarge? Ty hoardin' all the Pork and Beans?"

Ragatz laughed. "Good to see ya."

Ty got out the C-ration cookies he'd been saving and poured some tea. "VC tea, it's all we got, Dan."

"Fine with me."

Ty held up the cigarettes that came with the C-rations. There were unfiltered Lucky Strikes or King-sized unfiltered Pall Malls. Dan pointed at the Pall Malls, and Ty tossed him the four cigarettes in their little red box. He lit up the Pall Mall and relaxed as it hit him.

"What ever happened to the Kools, Ty?

Ty laughed, "Well Dan, I figure these C-rats are from either WWII or Korea. Nobody's been smoking unfiltered Lucky Strikes since you guys used to roll 'em up in your shirtsleeves. It's fucked up sending a brother over here with no Kools."

"So why'd they stick you guys out here?"

"We're both getting short an' they think Ty's Dinky Dao," Ragatz said, laughing and making the sign for crazy in the head.

"I am Dinky Dao Sarge. Send me home!" Ty said, waving his arms.

They were all laughing. Hell, who in this war wasn't Dinky Dao?

"You short Dan?" asked Ragatz.

"I'm over the hump, but I don't count the days. I just get uptight thinking about it, and besides it doesn't do any good."

They ate and smoked and complained about the food.

"How long you been out here?" asked Ragatz.

"Since before the Tet."

"Alone like this?"

"Had a partner, good guy, didn't make it." He paused and looked at the dirt. "Funny thing is, he was a better Seabee than I'll ever be."

Ragatz nodded his head, "Know what you mean. Seems to be the way it goes sometimes. The good ones don't seem to make it somehow. I don't get it."

Dan stared at the end of his cigarette.

Ty shook his head, "Maybe they're just good at the wrong things."

Chapter Twenty-Four

A few days later, Dan stood by the graveyard in Hoa An. The morning air was still relatively cool, the village was quiet, and he was supposed to meet one of the elders.

A man Dan recognized as Ong Thai emerged alone from the bamboo. Dan turned to greet him, and they bowed as peers, crossing their hands at the elbows. Although he was younger than the other elders, Ong Thai was usually included when important decisions were made. He was always neatly dressed, and Dan never saw him without his white cotton fedora.

He signaled for Dan to come with him. "Come school. You see new school."

Ong Thai's English wasn't any better than Dan's Vietnamese so, as they had no one to interpret, they took their time walking together, taking care to understand. Listening carefully to one another, their thoughts and feelings focused on their concern for the village and its way of life.

The sounds of the village and the immediate cares of the day began to fade into the background. The differences in their two cultures became less and less important as the urgent truth of their hopes and fears merged into a quiet, certain place they shared.

Dan respected Ong Thai because he never failed to act with sincere concern and care for the village and the people in it. He was always serious. Dan had never seen him laugh or even smile. It seemed as if Ong Thai could see the vast horror of the war hanging over the village like a giant hammer poised to smash his home, his family, his way of life, everything he had ever loved.

The trail through the bamboo opened into a clearing. Ong Thai stopped and gestured with his open hand. "Nha troung," (schoolhouse) "We make."

It was a small, one-room schoolhouse, lovingly made from lumber Dan had salvaged and hauled to the village in his truck. The villagers had very carefully fit the different pieces of the plywood puzzle together to make a school they were proud of.

Stepping inside, Ong Thai used his pocketknife to probe the joints and show Dan how carefully they had been fit together. "See, no sun, no sun."

Dan stood amazed at the work and dedication evident in the humble little schoolhouse. Beaming with pride, Ong Thai held Dan's hand as they walked back out into the sunshine and stood looking at the new school.

Dan was aware that this part of the village was closest to the road and was bordered on the south by an area that was controlled by deserters, warlords and criminal gangs. He sensed that this little school symbolized these people's unwavering commitment to a decent life in the face of the worst kinds of chaos just outside their door.

Ong Thai gestured with his palm down for Dan to follow, leading him on down the trail toward the southern border of the village.

The bamboo gradually fell away, opening to a large, irregular meadow where the trail curved around a low, grass-covered mound. The trail dropped away on the other side to reveal the twisted, ruined body of a young American soldier. He was laying awkwardly, face down, his hands tied behind his back. A gunnysack was tied over his head, covering his face that was turned away and down into the grass as if he were sleeping.

Dan looked around the edges of the meadow, the bamboo. Who had done this? Who were they? Where were they? Were they watching him now?

His vision narrowed until all he could see was the body in front of him. There was no sound. He felt drunk, the kind of drunk he wouldn't remember. He tried to walk but couldn't feel his feet. The ground felt hard and slippery. He was cold inside, not angry, not afraid, but stunned, curious, frozen in place.

Who? Why? What could this person have possibly done to deserve such a death?

He took a deep breath and stumbled across the mound and knelt beside the body where the blood and bodily fluids had soaked into the earth. It hadn't yet started to smell of rot, but it wouldn't be long. Using the sharp tip of his knife Dan pulled the blood-soaked shreds of the gunnysack away from the boy's face. The eyes and eyelids, ears, lips and nose, the tender parts, were gone, leaving only the teeth marks of the rats. Ong Thai came to his side and speaking in quiet, precise Vietnamese told him what the villagers had seen from the bamboo. Dan didn't understand the words, but somehow he understood what the man was saying.

The gunnysack had been stuffed with a couple of the big, hungry rats that had grown fat and aggressive on the greasy by-products of the war. Then the bag of rats had been tied over the man's head.

Against his will, Dan couldn't help but imagine the rats biting, clawing, chewing while the soldier ran, frantically shaking the bag on his head, trying to throw them off, the frenzied rats feeding on his eyes and then on through the eye sockets and along the optic nerves into the tender, sweet tissue of the brain.

There was a small clump of bamboo on the mound that had been cut at an angle, leaving sharp ends sticking out of the ground, and at some point the man had impaled himself on the sharp ends of the cut bamboo, driving it through the gunny-sack, through his eye socket and into his brain. It was hard to tell if he was trying to kill himself or the rats that were eating him alive, or maybe both.

After gorging on the sweet meat of the brain, the rats had gnawed their way out of the gunnysack and waddled away through the grass.

Standing up, Dan swallowed his disgust and his fear. He took a deep breath and looked around the clearing, the sweet M16 a certain comfort in his hand. He and Ong Thai stood over the body, looking at each other for a long time, trying to understand.

In his mind, he could see the Beast of War with its dogs of hell and army of rats in a dark cloud of blood lust over the land. Bloated and arrogant, it waited patiently with a bloody grin, knowing it had already won.

Dan stepped back and shook his head. "Who did this?" He asked, pointing to the head, the body, the bloody gunnysack. He was somehow detached. It was all like a movie, a horrible black and white "second feature" that he would have to get out of his head before he could ever go to sleep again.

Ong Thai looked at him until their breathing slowed in unison. He lifted his gaze away from Dan to the edge of the meadow then slowly around to each clump of bamboo, each mound of grass, each dark shadowed recess where someone could be watching.

"People watch... people say... numba ten GI."

"Deserters?"

Ong Thai nodded, "Numba Ten GI."

Ong Thai looked north, toward where the trail came into the clearing from Hoa An.

"People watch, people see."

Ong Thai turned toward him, eye to eye. "You too much alone Dan-i-el. Bad people, bad people do this."

Dan took Ong Thai's hand and held it, bowing his head, wondering, how could anyone do such a horrible thing? How could they even imagine it?

He shuddered as death's black hand brushed the back of his neck.

Chapter Twenty-Five

Dan knew Ong Thai had wanted him to see the miracle of the little school that the villagers had created from the scrap wood he had carried to them in his truck. Dan also understood that Ong Thai had wanted to warn him of the danger he was facing when he came into the village alone.

They left the deserter's ruined body and walked back up the trail. They stopped for a moment where the brave little school, full of dreams and promise, stood alone to hold back the chaos.

Ong Thai led Dan back to where the trail began a slow curve toward the graveyard. They stopped at a home that had been framed from the stalks of the bamboo and covered with the leaves in the old way. It was carefully made, inviting and clean with its hard-packed dirt floor and every small thing in its place.

Ong Thai asked him in. He poured the tea that had been made that morning. They drank together, measuring their common language deficits and regretting that they could not share more of what was so urgent and so dear to both of them.

Dan had the thought that maybe it was better that he and Ong Thai couldn't express themselves too well. He had no idea what he could have said.

When it was time to go, Ong Thai carefully cleaned the cups and placed them back where they belonged. Believing that this was Ong Thai's home, Dan wished him goodbye and started to leave, ducking out though the small door. Ong Thai followed him down the trail. Confused, Dan asked him if he were going to stay at his home. Ong Thai shook his head and said, "No, not my home."

Dan was taken aback. It hit him that he had just broken into someone's home, in a village on the other side of the world, where he was a stranger and a guest. He was concerned that he had committed a crime, made a major blunder, or at the very least offended the family who lived there.

"What about the people who live here? What will they think?"

Ong Thai pressed his hands together as he bowed and said, "They will be honored."

In some strange way, the little school house and Ong Thai's comment that the owners of the humble home would "be honored" seemed to offer an unforeseen sense of balance to the horror contained in the bag of rats.

Dan knew he could not abandon these people or the work he was doing in the village. He thought about the people at the Med-Cap, the children with the infections and wounds that would never heal.

There were so many lives, grandmas and grandpas, mothers and fathers all trapped in their quiet, desperate struggle to survive the atrocities of this war they had never asked for. How could he leave them? Again he thought about the little schoolhouse the people had built with so much care.

He thought about his great-grandfather who had left his young bride and newborn child to fight in all four years of the American Civil War. He thought about his mother and father who had never mentioned the word duty, but without complaint, did their duty to their family and their community every day of their lives.

There was no flag of battle in this war and no one to pick up the flag if he fell. He hadn't asked for it, but it was his duty to make the best of it. That was clear.

So he went back to the village the next day and the next and the next. He went back to the terror of the bag of rats, impatient for his ears, his lips, his eyes. He crossed that thin boundary into the village, swallowing his fear, pushing it down, pounding it deep into his guts and holding it there, the price of admission each day.

Chapter Twenty-Six

Dan wanted to see his teacher. He turned at the school, crossed the ancient railroad tracks and parked the truck. As he crossed the dirt yard to the front steps Chaplain Hu met him. He bowed, took Dan's hands in his own and said. "Ong De no here. He go Saigon. Mother sick."

Dan thanked him and turned to go.

The priest gestured to him. "Come me. I go ARVN base. You come." He said smiling, eyes flashing, and held up his hands like he was driving. "Take jeep!"

Robe and sandals flapping in his excitement, he ran to get the jeep. Before long, Dan heard him coming around the building, chugging along on full choke.

The priest bounced up and down on the seat, motioning for Dan to get in. He drove through the gate, shoved in the choke, and entered traffic at full speed without looking either way.

With no visible concept of vehicle code regulations, Chaplain Hu claimed the exact center of the road as his own. Smiling like a child, he gunned the old jeep along at full speed, sailing serenely down the middle of the road.

The ARVN (Army of the Republic of South Vietnam) base had the look of something that was forever out of place. It was not really Asian, and not really American. Rusty sagging wire ran alongside a dusty, unpaved road up to an almost deserted main gate.

To Dan, it looked like the Vietnamese Army was just going through the motions until the Americans left and the VC and the NVA finally took over. From what the Vietnamese had told him, the historical migration had always been from north to south, so it only seemed natural to them that the north would again prevail.

While proud of their national history, all the Vietnamese he had talked to had never used the words "communist", "VC", or anything remotely political. They had told him they appreciated the Americans efforts to help them, but realized that the Americans would leave someday. Most of them didn't even know where the United States was. As near as they could imagine, it was maybe somewhere on the other side of the Philippine Islands.

Chaplain Hu stopped the jeep outside the gate and said something Dan didn't understand. He left Dan in the Jeep and swept into the base as if he owned it.

Dan sat up and checked his sweat-stained cap and sorry uniform. He hoped he looked like an American official of some vague, undefined importance. He had no idea what Chaplain Hu was looking for, but he didn't seem especially pleased when he returned. Chaplain Hu started the jeep, found a forward gear, and turned the jeep around. They rattled through the gate and turned east toward Da Nang. The good priest was the same intense and focused person Dan was used to, but he drove more slowly and on his side of the road. To Dan, it seemed that his joy in driving the jeep had somehow been diminished by his encounter with the Army.

They crossed the Da Nang River and drove through the old, unchanged port district of broken buildings and hopeless, soiled water. Passing through Da Nang's downtown, Dan could see the colorful signs in large Vietnamese letters. He almost understood some of the words before they disappeared and others took their place. There was a camera shop with a Kodak sign, and a theatre marquee advertising The Pink Panther. There was a sign for Beer 33, another for Tiger Beer, and of course Coca-Cola.

He wondered what Lilly would think of it all. There were no military vehicles he could see, and except for a few Honda motorbikes and pedestrians, the streets were quiet and seemed almost normal, as if for today, the war was somewhere else.

Having exhausted the meager range of both their languages, he and Chaplain Hu drove quietly through the back streets of Da Nang through neighborhoods of quiet homes and little market places. The ancient jeep's tired engine purred through the empty streets.

He smiled at this good man, this fierce warrior for good. The Chaplain raised his eyebrows and patted the jeep's dashboard. The heat gauge was in the red and there were tiny wisps of steam escaping from under the front of the hood. Dan looked at Chaplain Hu, but he seemed totally unconcerned.

They rolled on until Chaplain Hu angled the jeep across the street and stopped in front of a four-story building that looked like it was part Buddhist temple and part headquarters for church business.

Chaplain Hu parked and turned off the engine. He slid out of the jeep and motioned Dan to come with him. The overheated motor was still turning, dieseling first one way and then the other until it wheezed itself into top-dead-center and stopped on the compression.

Entering through a side door, Chaplain Hu spoke to the humble monks with their robes and shaved heads, hurrying to obey his wishes. Climbing three flights of stairs, they entered a large room, where Chaplain Hu sat down cross-legged on a mat and motioned for Dan to sit across from him. Waiting in silence, Dan felt like he was where few, if any, Americans had ever been.

He reflected how for the first few months in Vietnam he had only been able to see his experiences in Hoa An through the thick bifocals of life from the narrow, dualistic perspective of Western Civilization. No matter how hard he tried, life in the village did not conform in any way with what he had been taught about the world and his place in it. Since he couldn't change the events, the dissonance of those experiences continually pulled him off balance, gently challenging everything he believed to be true.

He had tried to shoehorn the events in the village into the context of his previous life, but they didn't fit, and they weren't going to.

The monks brought food, and the good chaplain spooned the soup into two bowls, serving it first to Dan and then to himself. Dan lifted the soup to his face, savoring the exotic aromas and flavors.

In his bowl of soup there were two, tiny, pearl onions floating like small planets in the broth. He thought of himself and Lilly, small planets like the onions, drifting farther and farther apart.

Chapter Twenty-Seven

It had rained steadily for several days. Accompanied by the sounds of the rain beating on the tin roof, Dan had finally been able to sleep. The rain had stopped in the middle of the night and that morning he woke up to the news that soldiers in an Army convoy had shot and killed two small children playing by the side of the road. The big M14 rounds had torn their small bodies to pieces. One was dead, and the other lived a short time before dying.

Just as he was starting up the truck to go out to the village, Lt. McConnell walked up and put his hand on the open door saying, "The base is closed today Dan."

"Because of the shooting?"

McConnell nodded. "Yeah."

"Was it in Hoa An?"

"No, it was next door, just north of there."

Dan rested his head on the steering wheel. "I better go."

McConnell looked at him.

"I gotta be out there today Lieutenant. What'll they think if I don't show?"

McConnell nodded and gently pushed the truck's door shut. "Take care of yourself Dan. This is shit."

"Yeah, it is." Dan agreed. He reluctantly slipped the truck into gear and slowly eased it down the hill and out the gate.

The rice fields were full of water, and the roads and trails were wet and slick. The leaves of the bamboo dripped onto the soaked earth, making it sound like it was still raining. The whole world was wet.

He pulled the truck into the village then stopped and waited. A couple of elders came slowly, picking their way through the standing water.

There weren't any smiles. Their mood was serious, and he could tell they were upset. So was he. He felt small and helpless and somehow soiled by the whole thing. He got out and stood by the side of the truck. No one spoke. Dan looked down at the mud in frustration, grief, and anger. They waited until he looked up then stood looking into each other's eyes, trying to understand what made no sense. There was no interpreter, which was probably good because there were no words for what had happened.

After a while, they explained to him that a woman had given birth at the Aide Station the night before. The trails were flooded and impassable on foot and the elders were hoping Dan could take the parents and their new baby to their home in his truck.

It seemed like a simple enough request, and he welcomed the opportunity to do something of value.

The villagers carefully helped the woman climb onto the big seat. Wrapped in the wonder of their precious newborn, the proud father handed the baby up to her, and then joined them in the truck.

Dan drove slowly and carefully through the soaked earth and standing water, trying to miss the bumps and holes. He realized the father was directing him to a remote hamlet where he had never been. Because of the rain, the only route was through the middle of the neighboring village where the two children had been shot and killed that morning.

What started out as a wet, muddy road soon narrowed into a wet, muddy trail. The truck banged against the dripping bamboo on both sides, forcing the already angry villagers off the trail and into the brown, dirty water. Their eyes showed hurt, anger, confusion and sadness. He knew that each child was embraced and loved by the entire village and that everyone there mourned the two little ones as if they were their own.

He took some comfort as long as the mother and the father and the baby were with him in the truck. They arrived at a clearing in a remote part of the village where he had never been. The parents bowed, thanked him and left, holding the baby carefully as they walked the wet trail to their home.

Leaning against the truck, he realized that now he was alone. He wished he had a Pall Mall, but there were only four to a pack in the C rations, and he hadn't had any for a while. He thought about a conversation with his friend Smith who was from a small town in rural Georgia.

They had been discussing the differences in their home states and Smith had told him, "With those California plates on your car, you wouldn't make it from one end of my home town to the other."

Smith had just said it as a matter of fact. He didn't condone or condemn it. He was just telling it like he knew it to be. Dan wasn't sure exactly what he meant by "not making it from one end to the other," but he knew it wasn't anything too good.

Standing alone by the truck, he became increasingly apprehensive about driving back through the grieving village by himself. He considered leaving the truck and hiking cross-country to the base on foot. But he knew there would be mine fields on the way and that the Battalion would never forgive him for leaving one of their trucks in the middle of nowhere.

He was relieved when one of the elders, stepping carefully through the slippery mud, appeared at the edge of the clearing. Ong Trong was older than the other elders and always dressed in traditional, all white, loose baggy pants, thin jacket and little white skullcap. He had long white hair and a thin goatee tapering to a point under his chin.

Dan had met with him before and had always admired the way he carried himself and the way he treated everyone with wisdom and gracious humor. He fit Dan's image of a mandarin and at the same time reminded him of his own father, who possessed the same gentle humor and easy grace with others.

One of the villagers arrived with the tea. He and Ong Trong sat on a stack of handmade concrete blocks under a tarp that had been slung overhead to keep off the rain. Although Ong Trong didn't speak or understand a word of English, one of the boys soon arrived to interpret.

Dan sat looking at his jungle boots in the mud. How was this going to end? He and Ong Trong were having tea and talking together like it was just another day, but it wasn't. Finally, even though he felt foolish, he looked at Ong Trong, and asked, "Why am I still alive?"

The boy interpreting listened carefully then relayed his question to Ong Trong. The old man shook his head like he didn't understand.

Dan asked again. "Why haven't the villagers taken out their anger on me? The children were shot and killed by the American soldiers. I look the same as they do."

He pointed to his shirt. "I wear the same uniform. I came here through their village, and I will have to go back the same way."

Ong Trong crossed his thin legs at the knee and pouring the tea into each cup, he looked at Dan with eyes full of wisdom, and understanding, and what could have been affection of the old and wise for the young and foolish.

He spoke softly. The boy listened carefully then said, "We understand."

Seeing Dan's puzzled look, Ong Trong paused, then spoke again. While Dan couldn't understand the words, he could almost sense the meaning. When the boy translated it was as if the old man were speaking to him. "We understand Dan-i-el. There are good Americans, and there are bad Americans."

That was all he said. Holding on to the old mandarin's statement that *we understand*, Dan low-geared it back up the muddy trail through the grieving village by himself, the truck banging against the wet bamboo. He could see from their faces that the people were very unhappy, but they did not harm him, or curse him, or threaten him in any way.

He thought about a young American soldier remarking that the Vietnamese were ignorant because they did not have flush toilets. He thought about Smith telling him that he "wouldn't make it through" his hometown in Georgia with those "California plates" on his car. He thought about the men who thought it would be a good idea to send him to Watts to "knock heads" with an axe handle.

He could not help but wonder who was really ignorant and who was really civilized in this place and what in the world we were doing in this country, to these people, and why.

Slowly sloshing through the mud and pools of brown water, the truck waddled over the mounds and through the deep, wet holes, back through the unfamiliar village. Dan finally turned right on to the main road and started back toward the base. The sun had come out and the surface of the road was beginning to dry.

Making another right turn, he came face to face with a long line of serious vehicles of war trailing black diesel smoke. A full battalion of intense South Korean troops streamed down the middle of the narrow road, straddling the centerline, running everyone off on both sides.

The whole thing just rubbed him the wrong way. He didn't appreciate bullies, and after this morning he'd had enough. He wasn't about to be run off the damn road in his own damn village.

Holding the steering wheel with his left hand he aimed the mud covered International dump truck with the red "Yuan Su Vu" (Civic Action) sign, directly at the lead jeep of the convoy boss.

At the same time, he grabbed his forty-five in his right hand and rested it across his left arm and out the driver's side window.

The convoy boss was standing up in the back seat of the lead jeep. He saw the truck coming straight at him and then the gun. His eyes got huge and he started barking orders. The driver yanked the jeep back on the right side of the centerline, and like a big snake, the rest of the convoy followed.

It was a stupid thing to do and Dan knew it. He felt like he was losing it. He felt like he was *going bamboo* past the point of no return now, and there was nothing he could do about it. He could feel that there wasn't much left of who he had been and at the same time realized that what was left of him wasn't making a lot of sense.

Straddling the two worlds so impossibly different without a solid footing in either one, he was desperate for the sweetness of a woman's touch, but he knew that was not part of this deal.

He missed Lilly, but America had become another planet and he did not miss it. Although Lilly never left his mind, the constant barrage of intense experiences, the uniqueness of everything he encountered in the village and even the constant heat had stretched his memories of her thinner and thinner until he could not even remember what she looked like.

Chapter Twenty-Eight

Hoa An was his home now, and nobody was going to run the people off the road if he could help it. Confused and angry about the day's events, Dan parked the truck outside the gate at the Bo De School and walked in. Ong De met him at the steps to the main building and led him to the veranda. One of the teachers brought tea and gently placed it on the table.

They talked about the children who had been killed by the American soldiers that morning. Ong De was aware of what had happened, and like Ong Trong, seemed to share the wisdom that there are "good Americans and bad Americans." But Dan was hurt and angry and ashamed of his country and of his race. Looking for answers, he studied the random cracks in the concrete floor beneath his feet.

Ong De silently poured the tea. The shouts and laughter of the children playing reached across the courtyard. Dan wondered about the children who had been killed. One minute they were playing by the road, and the next they were gone. Maybe they had been laughing too, smiling and waving at the soldiers in the trucks as they rolled by.

Dan let out the breath he had been holding since that morning and said, "I don't understand it. How could anybody do that? They were just little ones."

Ong De nodded.

"It is just so wrong," said Dan. He was angry and disgusted and at the same time afraid that in some horrible way, he was no different. He wore the same uniform, spoke the same language, and came from the same part of the world. What atrocity could he commit without thinking?

He looked at Ong De and asked, "How can it be?"

Chin in hand, Ong De looked at him, waiting for the right words. Dan thought of Ong Trong stroking his chin whiskers that morning at the little school. He thought about how, in the same way, the two men seemed to regard him with kindness and understanding across time and distance.

He hoped Ong De would tell him a story that would somehow make everything okay. Instead, he poured more tea and asked, "Do you remember little Do Ti Thuan, her father, the men who killed him, the grandfather hit by the truck driver and the men who bought the scholarships?"

Dan looked at him without understanding.

Ong De asked, "Are they not all a part of the same story?"

Dan nodded and said, "It's like you wrote it, made it up and put it together, and somehow all it became real."

"And did you not have a part also?"

"I hadn't thought about it that way. I was just doing my duty, doing what I could."

Ong De nodded and asked, "In the story of Do Ti Thuan and the scholarships, are we not all connected, even you?"

Dan shrugged, "I guess so."

"So in this story, this sad story of the children by the side of the road waving to the soldiers, are we not part of it also?"

"I'm not the same as the guys that did that!" Dan protested, clenching his fists and staring at the floor.

"No, not the same, but still a part of the whole."

"Those kids didn't deserve it."

"No, of course not."

"I mean, think about it. They were innocent, just playing by the side of the road."

"Yes."

"And then there's the soldiers who shot them from the truck – target practice! And they just went on, never looked back!"

Dan stretched his clenched fists apart. "This isn't like the story of Do Ti Thuan!" he cried. "The children are dead! The soldiers are gone to who knows where! No matter how hard I try I cannot make sense of it."

Ong De said. "Please keep your hands apart in that same way. I'll be right back."

Curious, Dan held his hands apart, waiting until Ong De returned with a paper tablet. He sat it on the table and carefully poured more tea. He then asked, "What happens to your arms when you hold them out like that?"

"They get tired."

Ong De nodded and drew a straight horizontal line across the paper and asked, "What does this represent to you?"

"I don't know."

Ong De added a point, like an arrowhead at each end, pointing in opposite directions and asked, "What does it feel like?"

Dan looked at his hands, still apart, and said, "It feels rigid and tense. It brings up feelings of conflict, separation and isolation. It makes me tired, yet I can't seem to let go. I feel stuck."

Ong De reached over and pushed his hands farther apart. "What do you feel now?"

"Frustration, fear and anger. It's worse." He slammed his hands together.

"And now?

"Confusion."

Ong De pointed to the line. What if we put life at one end and death at the other?

Dan nodded. "Or good and evil, rich and poor, happy and sad, male and female, young and old. It goes on and on, the saved and the damned? The sheep and the goats? The chosen and the unchosen? The clean and the unclean?"

Ong De didn't say anything. Dan took a deep breath and looked up into the bamboo arching over the veranda and cried, "What's the point of it? Where does it end?"

The teacher poured more tea and said, "Shall we go on?

Dan nodded and said, "Please."

Ong De pointed at the paper. "We were talking about the line with the two extremes in conflict, pulling against one another. Stretching until it breaks, the center cannot hold and the meaning of it, the concentrated energy of it, shatters or collapses in on itself."

Dan let out the breath he had been holding and said, "It looks like chaos, war, children being shot in the streets for no reason."

Ong De nodded in agreement, offered the pencil to Dan and said, "Now make a circle on the paper."

Dan took the pencil and drew a circle on the paper below the straight line.

"Are you more relaxed now? Is there less pain, less anxiety?"

Dan took a breath, let it out and said. "Yes, very much so."

"Now imagine taking the circle on both sides and *twisting* it until it crosses in the center making two smaller circles, one in each hand. When it is clear in your mind, please draw what you see on the paper."

When he was done drawing Ong De asked, "What do you see?"

"The infinity sign?"

"Could be." Ong De smiled and asked, "Now, what do the two smaller circles represent?"

Dan wasn't sure. "The two sides of infinity?"

"And what else?"

Dan shook his head, "I don't know. Life and Death?"

Ong De leaned forward and asked, "Could it also represent the presence, or the influence, of time, or experience, perhaps the process of living in the river of each day?"

"Ah, so the circle reduces the tension of the straight line but is relatively stagnant, maybe spinning, but going nowhere."

Ong De shrugged. "Perhaps. See where the two circles touch, or cross?"

"Yes."

"Could that point of contact represent what we call life, or maybe consciousness?"

Dan thought of how he felt when he was with Lilly, the warmth from her touch, the way he felt when she kissed him. He closed his eyes to feel the truth of it. After a moment he looked up and said, "That makes sense."

Ong De smiled, paused and said, "Now make another drawing so that the two smaller circles are sketched loosely one on top of the other, so that they appear to be overlapping."

There it was, a symbol common to Asia. He had seen it on the flag of South Korea. Dan leaned back in his chair and asked, "What does it mean?"

The good teacher looked out over the schoolyard. The children were in class now and it was quiet.

Ong De spoke quietly, "Like any symbol, it can mean different things to different people at different times. It may mean one thing to me sitting on this side of the table or something different to you on the other."

"And both are true."

The teacher nodded and smiled at the student. "The important thing is what does it mean to you."

Dan could almost see it, but the teachings he had been raised with, every book, every movie, every story, every commercial rose up in his mind to block his understanding.

He asked, "Is that what we call Yin and Yang? How is it different from life and death, good and evil?"

"What do you see?"

"I can see how the energy flows back and forth between the two sides." Dan paused and asked, "Could the boundaries be made so the energy can pass between the two sides like the membrane between the mother and the child in the womb?"

Ong De nodded and said, "Sometimes I see it as the fish in the water, male and female, swimming in the moving river, flowing together in a dance, always changing but always connected in the cycle of life. See where they touch, or cross? That is where the..." He paused, looking for the right words.

Dan interjected. "The energy?"

"Yes, you could say it that way. Or, the feelings, are shared, and changed, changing each other, back and forth."

Dan nodded, finally beginning to understand. "It's more of an exchange of energy, feelings, beliefs and thoughts, like you and I are doing right now!"

"Yes!"

"But staying in balance, one side with the other?"

"Yes!"

"Always?"

"Yes!"

Ong De smiled at him and went on. "Like our big truck driver buying the scholarship for Do Ti Thuan. Good and evil, male and female, young and old becoming one, life and death becoming one also."

Dan thought for a moment then again held up his hands stretched apart and asked, "And the other way? The straight line? What happens to them, the two ends? Can they ever come together?"

Ong De shook his head. "They push away from each other, more and more away."

"Repelled, like two magnets."

"Yes."

"And it becomes harder and harder, right?"

"Yes. And when they can no longer bear being pulled apart, there must be a tragic crisis to release the energy and the ends suddenly collapse back toward the center, causing the chaos of violence, injury and death."

He paused to take a sip of tea, then went on. "But you must understand that each time it happens, with each crisis, the energy of life is lost, and the whole becomes weaker, more afraid, more desperate, and so it starts all over again."

Dan said, "Like this war."

Ong De nodded.

Dan thought of the children, shattered and bleeding by the side of the road and said, "The sacrifice of the innocent."

"Perhaps," Ong De said with tears in his eyes as he reached across the teacups on the table and took Dan's hands in his own.

"Perhaps."

Chapter Twenty-Nine

Dan suspected that the Battalion had inherited their Vietnamese workers from the previous commands. He also suspected that Mai, like many others, had been hired as part of a relationship or a sexual favor to some long departed officer or lifer. Rather than traditional Vietnamese dress, she often wore European style clothing and make up that tended to make her look like a bar-girl, or prostitute.

Dan had been to morning chow and was on his way back up the hill when he saw Durwood dragging Mai down the hill to the Senior Chief's office by the main gate. Grinning, Durwood had her arm twisted behind her back, pushing her along.

He could tell she was frightened and in pain. She was holding back, dragging her feet, trying to find a way out of what she knew was waiting for her at the Senior Chief's office.

She looked at Dan for help. What could he do? The Senior Chief was the highest ranking enlisted man in the battalion, and it seemed to Dan that everybody else seemed to be turning a blind eye if they knew what was going on, but how could they not know?

Like he had told Hunter about the Pen Pals. No one wanted to hear about it. The command didn't seem to care, and no one else wanted trouble with the Senior Chief.

An older woman he knew as Ba Wi scurried along beside Durwood, chastising him in rapid-fire Vietnamese. When the three of them approached the Senior Chief's office, the door opened, and Dan saw the jungle boots of the gang of men waiting for her inside. Ba Wi stopped and backed away, shaking her head, still chattering in protest. Durwood shoved Mai through the door and kicked it closed behind him.

Dan stood helpless, disgusted by what he had seen and more disgusted by his inability to do anything about it. He tried to rationalize it to himself by thinking that somehow it was different since Mai dressed like a bar-girl. Maybe it was somehow different if she wore make-up and European clothes and flirted with some of the men from time to time. But he knew that wasn't the point at all.

Like Hunter had said, the Senior Chief was a bad old pervert who had the authority to do pretty much whatever he pleased. Today it pleased him to rape Mai. He had used her before, but today was going to be different. He would rape her with the other men in his office as his audience and then they would take their turn with her.

Ba Wi stormed back up the hill and passed Dan without looking at him. He could see she was angry and crying. Disgusted by his helplessness, he went to his truck and drove off the base. Like when he was a teenager cruising town with no particular place to go, he just wanted to drive, get away.

Turning up the hill, he rolled through the checkpoint at the First Marine Division. Leaving the Marine base, he circled north and then back down to the rice fields of the flat land below.

He couldn't stop thinking about what was happening to Mai in the Senior Chief's office. While he understood the imperatives of an occupying army, he also understood that while a Vietnamese woman may be a prostitute, she still was someone's daughter, niece, sister, wife, sweetheart, or mother.

He slowed, stopped the truck, and sat looking out across the bright green fields of rice, the emerald-green sea of new growth in contrast to the jade-blue mountains on the northern horizon. The colorfully decorated shrines seemed to bless each blade of rice as it grew.

He sat for a while, letting the blues and greens fill his eyes, letting the beauty of the earth, somehow wash away the grim truth of that poor woman's life. It made no sense. He felt weak and base and degraded by the actions of his countrymen.

A young boy emerged from the field and walked toward the front of the truck, smiling. He stopped by the open window, pointed at Dan's sign on the front of the truck, and said, "Yan Su Vu."

Dan nodded at him. The boy stopped smiling and held Dan's gaze. Dan watched as the boy's eyes changed into the eyes of a wise old man. The boy reached up and touched Dan's arm.

"Yan Su Vu Numba one."

Tears flooded Dan's eyes and he took a deep breath to get control of himself. The boy's old eyes never left his.

"You Okay GI." He patted his arm. "You Okay."

The boy let go of Dan's arm and walked away alongside the road. Dan watched him in the rear-view mirror until he turned and disappeared into the bamboo bordering the green, green field.

Dan started the truck and started drifting back toward the base. He entered through the side gate, parked the truck and went to the sick bay to see his friend Bobby Burden.

"What's up with the Senior Chief?" Dan asked.

"What do you mean?"

Dan told him about what he had happened to Ba Wi's friend, Mai.

Bobby shook his head and said, "Aw shit."

Chief Critchett was inventorying the meds in the pantry at the other end of the medical hootch and overheard the conversation. He stepped into the room, looked at Dan, shook his head in disgust and went back into the pantry. Dan asked if the Corpsmen ever treated the women who worked on the base.

Chief Critchett stuck his head out and looked at him over his glasses. "We're not supposed to, but we do what we can. It would be safest to bring her to a Med-Cap."

Dan told Bobby and Art about the Senior Chief intercepting the mail from the Pen Pals.

Bobby raised his eyebrows and said, "All I know is that we have been getting a lot of guys from his little group with the clap."

"Or worse," said Art from behind the partition.

"Yeah, or worse. They're coming back from RnR with some pretty strange shit on their dick. But that doesn't seem to stop them from going again, and again."

"Again and again? These guys are going on more than one RnR?"

Art laughed from the pantry. "Some are going two or three, or even four times."

Dan was stunned. "You been on RnR Bobby?"

"Nope, you?"

"Nope."

Dan walked up the hill to his hootch from the sick bay, thinking about the reality that he might not get an RnR at all. He and Lilly had dreamed, planned and written about it almost from the first day he found out he was going to Vietnam. He didn't expect that everything had to be fair, but this did not sit right.

The days went by with dirty looks from Durwood or one of the "gang" almost every time Dan went in or out the main gate. The Senior Chief sat with his feet on his desk, grinning while Durwood yelled "Gook lover! Gook lover!"

He checked his weapons. He hadn't seen Mai and wondered about what had happened to her. Smith would know. Dan found him in the chow line for lunch. Smith was the one person that never seemed to change in this mess and Dan was happy to see him.

Smith shook his head and looked at him sideways, "Hey man, you're in the shit now aren't ya?"

"Fuck 'em. You know what they did to that woman?"

"Yeah. There's been some scuttlebutt."

"What?"

Smith let out his breath in a long and low sort of grunt then said, "Ah hell Dan, they beat her up pretty good, knocked her teeth out an' dumped her up at the gravel pit where she's givin' two-dollar blow jobs. Lucky they didn't kill 'er."

Tight in his guts, Dan slumped back against the wall of the chow hall, took off his cap and rubbed the hair on the back of his head. He needed a haircut.

"Shit, aw shit, thanks for telling me."

"Watch yourself man. They don't like being messed with and they're pissed, pissed at you."

"Like I said, fuck 'em."

They were at the door to the chow hall but he'd lost his appetite. He drove up the hill past the gravel pit. He didn't see anyone. Turning around and coming back down the hill he had a better angle.

Mai was there, covered in dirty rags kneeling in front of a lean-to made from a poncho. She heard the truck and turned toward the road. Her face and hair were matted with the red dust and dirt of the place, her eyes wide, staring into madness and death, her toothless maw open in a silent cry.

Disgusted, he slipped the truck into neutral and let it roll quietly by and on down the hill.

He turned left at the intersection and drove past the burnt out provincial building where they had held their first Med-Cap. He wanted to talk to Ong De. He thought about what he wanted to say. Anger and disgust, helplessness and shame rose up inside of him as he shifted up through the gears.

He thought about the big truck driver and Ong De saying, *maybe now he feels bad inside, like you. Perhaps his feelings and your feelings are becoming connected.*

He remembered how everything had changed for the better and the truckers gave the money for the scholarships, and Do Ti Thuan and her sister were able to stay in school. But in some way Dan would never know, the old Papa-san still had to pay.

And this thing with Ba Wi and Mai was so much worse. The big truck driver was just stupid and thoughtless, but when he had the chance he had veered toward something better. The Senior Chief wasn't stupid. He was a twisted, sick, and mean old man who soiled and rotted everything he touched.

The hot, thick rage came up in his throat and he bit it back. He wanted to cry but gripped the wheel hard and cleared his head. He wanted his guns, the sweet, deadly M16 that tore off rounds smooth as a zipper, and the clunky old .45 with the slugs as wide as the button on a man's work shirt.

That poor woman, I should have put a round in her head and put her out of her madness and her misery. But he couldn't even do that much for her. He looked at himself in the truck's rear-view mirror and shook his head in disgust.

Chapter Thirty

Dan was walking to his little office when he heard a woman cry out. He turned toward the sound and saw Durwood dragging Ba Wi down the hill for her turn with the Senior Chief and the boys. She tried to run but, Durwood grabbed her by the arm and twisted it behind her back until she was bent over from the pain.

Ba Wi turned and looked at Dan. Even then, with her arm twisted behind her, she tried to smile at him.

He cried out to her, "Ah, Ba Wi!"

Durwood stopped and glared at Dan. Ba Wi quickly twisted away from him and holding her shoulder, stepped toward Dan.

"Chao An Dan-i-el."

Durwood glared at him and reached for her. She twisted away one more time.

Dan called out, "Ba Wi, I need to talk to you."

She wasn't sure of the English, but understood the tone of his voice. Durwood grabbed at her arm. Dan stepped between them and spoke sharply in Vietnamese.

"Toi khong noi ting Vietnam!" (I don't speak Vietnamese language.)

Durwood was confused. He wasn't sure what was going on, but he didn't like it. Dan waved him away, and said quietly to her, "Go to truck, Yan Su Vu truck."

Why couldn't he think of the Vietnamese word for truck? He pointed to his badge. Ba Wi stayed behind him, slowly backing away.

Then it was a stare down with Durwood, who finally turned and left shouting, "Gook lover! You're a gook lover!" over his shoulder as he scurried on down the hill to report Dan to the Senior Chief.

Ba Wi was waiting for him at the truck. He helped her into the cab and drove out the side gate. She was silent for a while, Then without crying or raising her voice she said, "I work here no more."

Dan nodded. She sat erect, no tears, looking out the windshield. "Senior Chief numba ten G.I. Dan-i-el. He mean to Viet Nam woman."

He looked at her and nodded. The truth of it twisted in his guts and he could not think of anything to say. After they were down the road a ways she asked, "Why you say you no speak Viet Nam?"

"Toi khong noi ting Viet Nam?"

She nodded, "You say no speak Viet Nam. You speak Viet Nam numba one."

"That's the only thing I know."

She looked at him smiling like he was kidding. He paused to make sure she understood.

"I say it so many times it sounds like I really do speak 'ting Viet Nam' but that's about it."

He could see she understood and was amused.

After a while he asked her where she lived. She looked around and pointed to the side of the road. "Stop here good."

He stopped the truck. She opened the door to get out then stopped.

"Cam on, An Dan-i-el, thank you." She paused and looked away. "I have son, like you. He good boy. He go war, like you, far way." She paused and caught her breath. "I see he no more. I hear he no more."

She didn't say what side of the war he was on and Dan didn't ask. She looked at him across the big seat.

"I work on base no more Dan-i-el. I see you no more."

I see you no more.

Leaning forward he rested his head against the steering wheel. He turned so he could see her.

"I am sorry Ba Wi, so sorry."

She nodded and slipped out of the truck, quietly closing the door behind her.

He watched her walk away, sandals flapping, holding her straw hat. She turned and smiled her beautiful smile. He waved and watched her disappear into the crowd.

Chapter Thirty-One

Slowing the truck down to enter the base, Dan saw the Senior Chief and a couple of his cronies gathered inside the office by the main gate. Someone yelled, "Gook lover!"

The Senior Chief was laughing with his feet up on the desk. "White Cong bastard! Plug that gook lover!"

Another one of the guys made the sound of firing a tommy gun, "Rat-a-tat-tat! Rat-a-tat-tat!"

He drove to his hootch and wrote a letter to Lilly. He didn't want to alarm her, but he needed her wisdom, her clarity.

When she wrote back, her letter was pretty clear.

> *Come home. I don't care what you have to do, but I want you to come home. This Chief may be mad at you, but you don't have to be mad at him. Don't play his game.*
>
> *I am proud of you and the work you're doing in the village. You've changed, and so have I, but you will never be like him. We have the rest of our lives to sort this out. Right now, I just want you home. I am waiting for you.*

Dan read her letter again that night, then finally dozed off thinking of her. He slept hard until the dreams of the black bag came for him out of the dark. Rats, big, black and hungry, bloody fangs gnashing like steel on the blade of a sword flew at his face, his ears, lips, nose and eyes, always the eyes. Their whiskers scratched across his face. The bag closed over his head.

He woke up, arms flailing, naked in the middle of the hootch, fighting, trying to tear off the bag, striking out with his hands, tearing the imaginary rats off his face and flinging them across the room.

Dan looked around. The other guys were sleeping. Peacock opened one eye, turned over and went back to sleep.

He felt like a fool. The mosquito net could keep out the rats at night but not the ones in his guts. They were already inside of him. He began staying up late, drinking coffee, prowling the perimeter, trying to push the dream cycle into the light of the next day. That worked for a while. Then it didn't.

He was standing in line for noon chow with the tin tray in his hands when his vision darkened until there was only a sliver of light around the edges. Everything else was black. All he could see was the black gunnysack of rats getting larger and larger, coming to be tied over his head. It was the same as the nightmare, but he was awake. He dropped the tin tray and didn't know it. The bag was closing over his head. The rats came for his eyes.

Peacock shook him. "You Ok?"

Dan turned and stumbled for the door, daylight! The rats swirled around his head. The darkness took over again. He leaned against the wall of the chow hall and slumped to the ground.

Peacock knelt in front of him.

"What's going on, Dan?"

He shook his head.

"Let's go to sick bay."

Peacock took him by the arm. Dan clung to him.

By the time they got to the sick bay it was starting to go away. Bobby Burden sat him down and watched him. After a while he asked, "Feeling better?"

"Yeah."

"What happened?"

"Don't know."

Bobby pursed his lips and handed Dan a cold orange pop. "Look Dan, orange pop is good stuff, but it's not a cure for everything."

Dan tried to laugh and stood up, pressing the cool glass bottle to the side of his head. Bobby and Mike were looking at him. Bobby asked, "Where you going?"

"Bo De School."

Ong De. He needed to talk to his friend.

Unsure of himself, Dan stopped at the gate of the Bo De School. No one came out to usher him in. No Ong De. He waited for a few minutes then walked on into the courtyard.

One of the teachers met him at the front steps.

"Ong De no here. He go Saigon, mother ill."

Chaplain Hu stepped out of the main building and looked down at him from the top step. Dan could see the good priest was burdened. He descended the three, four steps and took Dan's hands in his own, looking deeply into Dan's eyes. "You sad, you worry."

Dan shrugged and tried to smile. "Yeah."

"Want to see friend."

Dan nodded, "I do."

"He come back three days. You come then. We go ride in jeep!"

Dan smiled. He knew Chaplain Hu was trying to cheer him up. But he could tell the good priest was weighed down with his own problems. He suspected that the Buddhists were well informed throughout most of Asia. Chaplain Hu would know what was going on long before the Americans.

It struck Dan that the Americans might never know. It seemed like they didn't know, and didn't want to know. It seemed like they preferred to simply make up a narrative to suit themselves, their purposes, their reality, a reality that had nothing to do with him or the people of Hoa An.

"Come back three days. Ong De here three days."

Dan realized he was still holding the priest's hands in his own. He let go and bowed. They both smiled and almost laughed. Three days.

He decided to visit the Ty and Ragatz. The hike in to their camp was shorter than he remembered. It wasn't long before he caught the smell of American cigarettes and followed it on in.

He didn't know if they had booby-trapped the trail or not. He stopped and rattled the tin cans on the wire. "Hello in the camp."

"Hey, Seabee, come on in."

That was Ragatz.

"How'd you know it was me Sarge?"

"Well hell, you're the only one who ever comes to see us."

Dan laughed. "Doesn't your command ever come out?"

"No, does yours?"

"Not if they can help it."

Ty sat up from a nap, yawned and said, "Hell, I'm not so sure they even know we're out here."

Ragatz agreed. "The way I figure it, the Battalion's org chart said they needed to deploy a Civic Action Platoon so they sent me an' Ty out here to get us outta their hair."

"What do you mean? You guys are the most squared away Marines I know."

Ragatz nodded, "No shit, Dan. We are."

He and Ty saluted each other without sarcasm. "I guess we just didn't buy it anymore."

Dan wondered what Ragatz meant about not "buying it anymore." When he thought about it, he had to admit that whatever "it" was, he probably had never "bought it" either.

He asked Ty and Ragatz, "Did I ever tell you about the guy I picked up hitching into Da Nang to get his pay straightened out?"

Ragatz said, "Nope, but feel free to entertain us."

Ty smiled at him and said, "Go right on. Seabee. Tell us a story we haven't heard. Hell, or even one we have heard. We're not picky."

Dan had to laugh. "Okay. I was coming back up from Hoi An when I saw a Marine by himself by the side of the road. I didn't think he was a deserter but he seemed sort of out of place there by himself. All he had on was boots, shorts and a flak jacket. He was carrying an M16 and a sling with *beaucoup* magazines."

"Before I got the truck stopped he jumped in and shouted, *'Get the hell outta here! There's a sniper up in the tree line been takin' pot shots at me all morning!'*"

"I gunned the truck on down the road and when we were around the bend I asked him where he was headed."

"He told me he was on his way to Da Nang to see the disbursing clerks."

'They got my pay all messed up, and my Mom ain't getting her allotment, and she's gonna get

kicked outta her place. I don't want her homeless so I gotta get it straightened out!'

"I asked him if his Command could help him out with that."

'They can't find their ass with both hands, if you know what I mean. They sit around the O Club all night drinking and getting shit faced, and then they come up with these big ideas that just get us shot up and make no sense at all. That is, unless you're drunk too. Fucked up ain't it? You think I'm Dinky Dao, huh?'

"I told him I didn't think he was Dinky Dao and that nothing much surprises me anymore so he went on telling me about it."

'No shit, we tried it one time. We had a set of orders that had made no sense, almost got us killed. Someone had left a whole pallet of Carling Black Label just sittin' there outside the bunker, so we all started drinking it.'

"I asked him, a whole pallet, like with a fork lift?"

'Yeah. And the more we drank, the more those orders made sense. When we were all totally shit-faced, they were fucking brilliant. I shit you not.'

Ty and Ragatz both laughed out loud, but knew it was all too true. Dan had heard rumors of commanding officers who never made a decision without whiskey being involved. He has also heard of others who were never happy unless someone, it didn't matter who, was bleeding.

Ragatz asked, "What did you do with him?"

Dan shrugged, "Dropped him off at the corner back there on the road to Da Nang and wished him well."

Chapter Thirty-Two

Dan's tour was well past halfway over and there was no sign of an RnR on the horizon for him at all. With the Senior Chief handing out the RnR's to whomever, and for whatever reasons he pleased, it wasn't looking good for Dan.

From what he could tell, the guys who were married, or just wanted to see their families or girlfriends, were out of luck. The Battalion only had so many RnR billets, and the Senior Chief was saving them for his own purposes.

Dan had been more than busy, and he was starting to get "short" when all of this came clear to him. It looked like he wasn't going on RnR at all. He had just assumed they would be allocated fairly. Lilly and he had talked about it and written each other about it. It was the one thing they had to hang on to.

The more he thought about the Senior Chief and the RnR's the more disgusted he got. He didn't lose his temper or anything. He was just disgusted and had enough.

He knew that the Senior Chief crossed a small footbridge to go to his quarters at night and he went looking for him. He wasn't in his office so he went to the company office. The clerk, Charlie Davis, was a friend he had known from Hueneme.

Dan waited until there was no one else in the office then asked quietly, "Hey man, how do I get my RnR?"

"That's up to the Senior Chief."

"I know. And I know what's goin' on with him and his little friends."

Charlie didn't say anything.

"He's gotta cross the bridge to go to his hootch at night, right?"

Charlie nodded.

Dan said, "I'll be waiting for him at the bridge to cut his throat."

He hadn't thought about it, but it seemed like the right thing to do. The words seemed to come out by themselves.

Charlie looked up at him without expression, "Don't do anything stupid. Let me talk to McConnell."

Dan thanked him and went to sharpen his knife anyway. It still seemed like the right thing to do.

Chapter Thirty-Three

Chaplain Hu had said Ong De would be back from Saigon in three days, but three days came and went several times before Dan was able to return to the school and the shade of the veranda. Ong De poured the tea while Dan told him about the Senior Chief and what had happened to Mai and Ba Wi.

He told him about how he had convinced the truck drivers to take the salvaged lumber and roofing tin from the destruction of the base to the villages instead of the dumps. He explained how angry the Senior Chief had become and how he and his gang of followers had started calling him "White Cong."

He took off his cap and ran his fingers through his hair. "They say I am a traitor and love the Vietnamese people more than my own."

"I am proud of what my country stands for, but this isn't it. I'm ashamed, ashamed of people like the Senior Chief. He raped and almost beat Mai to death. He threatened my friend Ba Wi, and now he is threatening me."

"Why does he threaten you?"

"Because I tried to help Mai and Ba Wi. Because I know what he is doing, and because I interfered with his deal with the warlords at the dumps."

"So he has reason to dislike you."

Dan grunted, "And oh yes, I threatened to kill him."

Ong De rested his chin on his hand and looked at Dan across the table. Finally he nodded and asked, "Where you angry?"

"Not so much. I just had enough. He gave my RnR to one of his gang. I just had enough so I told his clerk that I would kill him."

"Did you mean it? Was that your intention?"

Dan nodded, "Yes, It seemed like a good idea at the time."

"What happened?"

"I got my RnR."

"When do you leave?"

Dan squinted. "Six days."

Ong De raised his eyebrows and asked, "So this Chief has many reasons to dislike you?"

"Yes."

Ong De asked, "So he is not like the big truck driver who could see a better way?"

"No, I don't think so."

"And you believe he will harm you."

"Sooner or later. "

Ong De leaned back and said, "Chaplain Hu and I have heard these things as well."

He looked at Dan across the coffee table and rose from his seat, "Come with me."

Ong De's room contained only a sleeping mat rolled against the wall, an armoire in one corner, and a small shrine. The hardwood floor was scrubbed and polished. There was only one small window at the far end. The room was almost dark. Dan stopped at the door and took off his boots.

Ong De sat cross-legged on the floor and gestured for Dan to do the same. He lit a candle and placed it on the floor between them.

"Are you afraid of this man, this chief?"

"Yes."

The flame wavered and almost went out. *Like the feeling in my guts.*

Ong De looked at him through the candlelight. "First, you must surrender to your fear."

The bag of rats rose up out of the darkness and came for him. He gagged, choked, and waved his arms in front of his face. He couldn't imagine surrendering to that.

He told Ong De about the rats. "They have taken over my dreams at night. I am afraid to go to sleep. Now they are coming for me in the daytime, when I am awake."

Ong De looked at him for a long time without saying anything. He matched Dan breath-by-breath, breathing slower and slower, staring into the flame. He spoke in a quiet voice. "Now you may lie on your back."

Dan felt safe here. The bag of rats seemed far away. Ong De spoke quietly, pausing to breathe. "Relax your fingertips."

Dan did as he was told. Ong De led him to relax his arms and his feet, his legs, his back, his neck, his mind.

"See the light from the candle on the ceiling. Take a deep breath and let it out slowly."

Dan did as he was told.

"Where is your fear now?"

His breath quickened. His stomach tightened and he gasped, "Huh!"

Ong De stroked the beard he didn't have, nodded and said, "Watch the light from the candle." He waited until Dan's breathing slowed. He spoke softly,

> "Imagine your feet like fish peacefully swimming in the river.
>
> Breathe.
>
> Imagine your hands like birds flying gracefully in the evening sky.
>
> Breathe.
>
> Imagine you are floating above the green earth.
>
> Breathe."

He waited. Dan's eyes closed. His breath slowed. Ong De went on, pausing, taking a breath, after each phrase.

"Let, the heavens calm you with their gentle light.

Breathe.

Feel the mounds of your chest separate. Feel them open and slide down away from your heart.

Breathe.

See a clear diamond of white light as it rises, from your heart, ascending to the heavens, joining God within – God without.

Breathe."

A warm, quiet darkness closed over him and he slept in peace. He didn't sense Ong De rise and slip out. He didn't sense Chaplain Hu look in on him.

Dan opened his eyes and watched the light of the candle dance around the ceiling. He didn't know how much time had passed.

He put on his boots and found his way down the stairs. Ong De poured the tea.

They sat on the veranda while Dan collected his thoughts. Finally he said.

"I am here with one foot, one part of my brain in the west where I grew up and learned everything I know, every thought about who I am and the very nature of my relationship with the world around me, as well as the very nature of my relationship with God. And I am here now with my other foot, another part of my myself here in Asia, where nothing is the same."

He paused and laughed, "Not only is it not the same Ong De, but many times it turns out the be the very opposite."

Ong De laughed and nodded his head, encouraging Dan to continue.

He told Ong De about when Ong Thai had invited him for tea in someone else's house and how he had become alarmed that he had committed a crime or offended the people to whom the home belonged.

Ong De asked, "And what did he say?"

"He said they would be honored."

Ong De nodded and poured the tea. "You struggle to understand these differences."

Dan laughed, "I do."

He looked down at the patterns made by the cracks in the concrete floor. No matter how many days he spent in the village, no matter how many customs he observed, or Vietnamese words he learned, he was still looking at life from his own point of view, the point of view of his experiences, his life in the western world. It was what he had been taught, all he had ever known.

Ong De smiled at him and said, "Perhaps it would be easier if you sat in my chair and I sat in yours."

As they laughed together, the grim seriousness of his convictions gradually loosened their grip on his heart. He could see that Ong De was familiar with both east and west. He had studied in Saigon and in Paris. He was as conversant with Socrates, Plato and Jesus as he was with Buddha, Confucius and the Tao. They were all equal to him, all worthy of his consideration.

Dan thought of the day in the village when he had asked to see the priests and the elders had said, "We have no priests."

He had asked them again and they had explained, "We have no priests. Each father is a priest. Each home is a shrine."

He looked at his wise teacher across the tea table. Ong De was quiet, waiting. Dan told him what the elders had said. "When they explained to me that each home is a shrine and each father a priest, it touched me. I understood what they said and what it meant to them and to me. I could see that each child, each blade of grass, each person was equal, valued and sacred."

Ong De nodded, listening.

Dan continued, "Somehow that moment changed how I see everything. It has changed how I see the world around me and how I see myself. It's how I want to live. It is how I want to be."

He looked at Ong De for encouragement. Ong De nodded his head and smiled. Dan sensed his approval.

Like the villagers, Ong De seemed to take what made sense, what worked in his life today. He seemed to accept the wisdom of both worlds, east and west, the truths that lasted, the truths that prevailed on the honest anvil of everyday life.

Chapter Thirty-Four

The clerk must not have cared for the Senior Chief any more than anyone else, because the orders for Dan's RnR came through in a couple of days. One day he was scraping the mud off his boots and the next he was in a big, sparkling clean, blue and white Pan American 707 with a smiling stewardess serving him a big steak. Then he was in Hawaii, and Lilly walked out of the crowd and into his arms.

They rented a little white Toyota and drove around Oahu, stopping at the empty beaches along the way. The next day they went to Kauai and did the same. There was so little traffic on Kauai that he and Lilly walked down the middle of the road holding hands.

A lady came over a hill in the distance walking slowly toward them. As she got closer, they could see that she was pushing a cart. They stopped and talked with her. She gave them sandwiches and fruit smoothies from her cart, but declined payment saying, "No please. This is my gift to you."

They were on Oahu when Neil Armstrong, Michael Collins, and Buzz Aldrin returned from walking on the moon. The astronauts orbited the earth, splashed down in the Pacific and steamed into Pearl Harbor to a hero's welcome.

"Do you want to go down and watch them come in?" Dan asked Lilly.

"No. This is just fine." She burrowed her curly blond head closer into his shoulder and fell asleep. Her closeness aroused him deeply, but he felt like a stranger in his own body. He wondered who he had become. He wondered if she knew him as he was with the mud and stink of the war still on him. He held her close while she slept, her beauty washing over him like a warm rainbow. He turned his face into her hair, remembering her scent like fresh apricots still on the tree.

He thought about when he and Lilly were newly married. They were living in a small upstairs apartment next to the freeway in San Luis Obispo when everything was changing around them. The 101 on-ramps were flooded with hundreds of young people hitching a ride to San Francisco.

His best friend, Mike "Suds", was home on leave from Army Officer Candidate School. He and Dan had grown up together, fishing the small coastal creeks for the wild trout and occasional steelhead. They had been friends in junior high school and high school and later roommates, working their way through Cal Poly.

Over six-feet tall, with a smile that never stopped, Mike was a friend in the very best sense of the word.

Dan and Lilly were at home in their apartment when Mike and his girlfriend, Sandy, burst through the front door. Mike held up the Beatles Sgt. Peppers Lonely Hearts Club Band album and said, "You've got to hear this! And, better yet, we're all going to Monterey Pop!"

It was the Summer of Love in California in 1967, and the Monterey Pop Festival was the celebration of that brief moment in human history when the promise of "do unto others as you would have them do unto you" and "all people are created equal," combined into a unique, fleeting moment of human possibility.

After Jefferson Airplane closed on Saturday night the crowd began filing out of the Fairgrounds while Booker T and the MGs were setting up. When they opened up with that clean, tight R&B groove, almost everyone who had left turned around and poured back in. The Marquees joined the band and started blowing for all they were worth. Otis Redding, who had just had a big hit with "Sitting on the Dock of the Bay" came out singing "I Been Loving You Too Long."

Everyone was on their feet dancing together. This was music you could dance to and everyone was dancing together. Long hairs and short hairs, grandparents and little children, black, brown, white, even the police danced with flowers in their caps. Everyone was dancing, dancing together, hoping it would never end.

But it did. By 1968, the major cities of the United States were in flames from New York and Detroit to Los Angeles. The war in Vietnam was reaching out and touching more and more young men and their loved ones through the draft. The violence of the war in Vietnam was mirrored by the violence against each other at home. The Summer of Love was over all too soon, and Dan was on his way to the war.

Chapter Thirty-Five

The rice fields dried out. The rhythms of war resumed with a tired monotony, while Dan continued to walk between the two worlds.

Leaving the mess hall one morning, he ran into Lt. Lawson, the Battalion's Intelligence Officer.

"Hey, Dan."

"Good morning."

"The S2 (Intelligence) at First Marine rang me up this morning and asked what's going on in the village."

Dan didn't know what to say. There was a lot going on. People were dying, babies were being born, life was continuing in spite of all the reasons it shouldn't. But Dan figured that wasn't the kind of information the S2 was looking for.

"We're doing Okay. The PFs do a good job of keeping the peace. The VC are in and out once in a while stashing weapons, but less and less now that we're doing the regular Med-Caps."

"So you would say we're making progress?"

"I would. It's always a dance, but yeah, I would. Hoa An is a decent place, and the corpsmen make a huge difference."

"And the people appreciate it?"

"They do. It's life and death for them, especially to the parents when their children are sick and they can't help them. You should see their faces when they see the Corpsmen coming in for a Med-Cap."

Lawson nodded.

Dan asked, "Why don't you come out with me sometime, Lieutenant?"

"Maybe I will."

Dan knew he wouldn't, but he would be welcome, and he would learn a lot more than he ever could from his office on the base. Lt. Lawson was one of the guys who had bought a scholarship for the children at the Bo De School. He was a decent guy and Dan had always liked him. He decided it was a good time to bring up the road project.

"There is something we should take a look at, though."

"What's that?"

"Well, the one thing they have asked help with is a road to connect the two hamlets in back with the two in front."

Lawson didn't say anything, but he was listening, so Dan went on.

"When it rains, the rice fields flood, and the two hamlets in back are cut off and isolated.

"They've asked for our help on it?"

"They have."

"What do you think?"

"Well, you know how it is. They'll never say it, but the fact is when they're cut off like that the back hamlets are isolated and wide open to infiltration."

"VC?"

Dan nodded.

"I see."

"Putting a road in there will do more good than anything else we could do."

"So what should I tell the Marines?"

Dan laughed, "tell 'em things are pretty good for right now, but it'd be better if we had a road."

While the Battalion still did not like the idea of leaving one of their precious bulldozers in the village, the military advantages of connecting the hamlets, framed around the threat of infiltration by the VC, finally seemed to make the difference.

One of the Civil Engineers came out to take a look at the site the elders had chosen. It followed the ancient trail from the graveyard across the rice field, angling slightly north toward the small elementary school on the other side.

The Engineer walked it off, trying to determine the capacity and placement of the big culverts that would carry the water under the road. At the same time, Dan could not help but notice some of the old farmers shaking their heads and muttering among themselves. Dan asked one of the boys what they were saying.

"They say pipes too small. They say bridge better."

"They look pretty big," Dan said, looking at the culvert halves.

"Big rain, *boucoup* water," said the boy shaking his head and pointing up the valley. It was dry now, but Dan could see the hills to the south and west that would be draining into the valley when it rained. He understood the elders' concerns.

He walked over to where the Engineer was looking up and down the rice field. After a polite interval Dan volunteered,

"The elders are thinkin' a bridge might be a better way to go."

"It might be, but we don't have a bridge. What we've got are culverts."

He stopped and looked at Dan to see if he understood. "We've got the culverts, Dan, and they are not going to be used for anything else so you can have 'em. How would you build a bridge in this mud anyway?"

Dan couldn't argue with that. It did seem impossible to try to build anything in this bottomless muck.

The culvert halves were delivered and they went to work bolting them together. The culverts were constructed of overlapping pieces of galvanized steel, each half-round piece making up a top or bottom of a section about three feet long and three feet in diameter.

Dan was pleased to actually be doing something and the work suited him. One of the elders spoke to one of the Popular Force boys.

The boy told Dan, "He say you no work."

Dan laughed and kept at it.

"He say you honcho, no work."

Dan laughed, took off his shirt, and went on bolting the culvert halves together. It felt so good to finally have his hands on something real, to actually be here, connected to something of actual and lasting value, to sweat and get his hands dirty.

But he could see that they weren't going to have it. One of the Mama-sans moved in laughing, teasing him, gradually pushing him out of the way until he gave in, picked up his shirt and raised his hands in surrender. Everyone had a good laugh at his expense and the work went on.

One of the elders was led to where Dan was standing and was introduced as Ong Wat. Dan bowed. "Chao Ong."

Ong Wat returned his bow then smiled and grabbed Dan's hands in his own that were rough and misshapen from a lifetime of hard work in the fields. His feet had also been shaped into the tools used to tend the water, the mud, and the soil, to grow the rice.

His face was so dark under his conical hat that all Dan could see was his shining eyes and broad smile.

Dan bowed his head again and repeated, "Chao Ong."

Ong Wat nodded and smiled, and held Dan's hands in his own.

When they finally started building the road, Ong Wat became the lead man, jumping in and organizing whatever needed to be done. His home was nearby, and he was always the first one on the job in the morning and the last one to leave at night.

Dan always bowed to him when they met. Ong Wat would return his bow grab Dan's hands, and laugh out loud. The road project began taking on a life of its own, and as the days passed, Dan found himself caring more and more for the old farmer who reminded him so much of his own father.

They both loved the land and understood the soil as alive with its own needs and wants and rewards. They also had the gift of approaching each task with unfailing good humor along with genuine pleasure and pride in their work.

One morning, Ong Wat and the others were waiting for him at the east end of the road. They were not working, but approached him with their hats in their hands, eyes on the ground, so distressed they couldn't speak. Dan could tell they had met together and had carefully discussed exactly what they would say.

An Son spoke for them, slowly and carefully choosing each word.

"Woman come from other village. She walk here last night. Take piece of big pipe."

"One of the culvert halves?"

"Yes." He said making the shape of one of the culvert halves. When he was sure Dan understood he continued.

"They are shamed and everyone in the village is shamed."

They still were not looking at him, and Dan could see they were mortified.

"They worry that you know, no person from Hoa An take pipe. Woman from other village, she take."

"I understand," said Dan nodding, "Please let them know I do not blame them."

An Son spoke to them, and they nodded that they understood, but they still would not look at him.

"Please tell them that I will try to find another piece as soon as I can."

No matter what he said they were inconsolable and work had stopped. Remembering Smith's advice, he drove in to a PX in Da Nang. He bought a pint of Old Crow and drove back to the base with it sitting like a little golden deity on the seat beside him.

He found the petty officer in charge of the Battalion's construction materials in the storage shed. He checked the name tag on the man's shirt. It said "Rodgers." He sat the Old Crow on a stack of lumber where the sun caught it just right.

"I hate to say it, but it looks like we're gonna need another culvert half."

"How come. Didn't you get what was ordered?"

"Yes." Dan paused, wishing he didn't have to say it, "but one got stolen."

"Stolen?"

"Yeah."

"Thievin' bastards."

Dan didn't say anything, but glanced at the bottle of Old Crow, wondering when it was going to start doing its part.

Rodgers said, "You know they're just makin' bunkers out there with those things, don't ya?"

"It wasn't anybody from the village who took it. It was a woman from another village who was passing through."

"A woman couldn't lift one of those things by herself. How do ya know it wasn't VC?"

"Well, because I believe 'em, Rodgers."

"You're nuts an' you'll get your throat cut. Ten to one the VC's got it now, making bunkers like I said."

"Maybe." Dan knew that one of the realities of this war was that in order to survive, every family had to have access to a bunker of some kind, some safe place, and the culvert halves did make a perfect entry.

"Go ahead," Rodgers said, picking up the bottle and slipping it out of sight. "You know where they are."

"Yeah, thanks. Enjoy the booze." He knew he shouldn't say anything, but he couldn't help himself.

"What booze? Rodgers grinned. "I don't see no booze."

The plan was to use the bulldozer to push the soil from the field into an elevated roadway that would be above water when it rained. But the field was soft and muddy. As soon as the Cat' took a bite it bogged down and sunk into the muck.

Another problem was Peterson, the equipment operator who came with the bulldozer. He was more interested in trying to meet the village women than building the road. There was no prostitution in Hoa An, and from what Dan could see the villagers had a well-defined, traditional sense of interpersonal relationships. It was explained to Dan that if a woman became a prostitute, her entire family would be shamed forever. In the worst case, they would be forced to abandon their ancestors. If a woman entered into a relationship with an American, it almost always resulted in either shame or a marriage in which the family was abandoned when the soldier went back to the "world".

A skinny guy with a little potbelly and a scraggly mustache, there was nothing especially attractive about Peterson, but in addition to his wife in the states, he seemed to have girlfriends everywhere. One day, he came to Dan with a letter from his wife.

"She says she's leaving me." He was appropriately downcast, but didn't seem too broken up.

"How come?"

"I don't understand it."

"Did you ever write her?"

"Nope."

"Maybe that's why."

"Do you think I should've?"

"Might've been a good idea," Said Dan, thinking of how long it had been since he had written Lilly.

The other problem with Peterson, however, was that he was just not a very good equipment operator and kept getting the big bulldozer stuck in the muck. As soon as he dropped the blade, she'd dig in and the tracks would dig deeper and deeper. He'd back up, try it again, and have the same results.

Even though they had finally been granted the precious bulldozer, the road was just a pile of mud at one end that didn't seem to be getting any longer. Dan was concerned because he knew the Battalion could assign the bulldozer to another project at any time.

No one seemed to know where he came from, or why, but one day an equipment operator from the Vietnamese Army Engineers showed up at the job site. He was a wizard with the big Cat'. He knew that if he slowed, stopped, or tried to take too big a bite, he would bog down and go nowhere. He never seemed to stop but ran full speed, just skimming the top layer of damp, soft soil with the blade, pushing it up to build the road and then backing away to do it again.

One day, he reported that he was running low on diesel fuel. Now that the bulldozer was on the site, the project had become substantially more official, and the next morning a small tanker truck squeezed its way down the trail.

At first they were elated that the tanker had arrived, then everyone saw the problem at the same time. The road was more than half way across the rice field now, and the small stream wandering through the saturated earth was between the bulldozer and the tanker.

Somehow they had to get the bulldozer across the stream to refuel it. The ground at the creek was especially soft and muddy, without a bottom of any substance.

Without saying anything, the new operator fired up the Cat'. He backed farther and farther away from the water. Giving it full throttle with black smoke billowing from the stack he charged the creek. It looked like he would be stuck for sure.

As the Cat' approached the creek, he dropped the blade and skimmed up a thin layer of earth. Reaching the stream, the operator never slowed down, but dropped the soil into the water and crossed the creek on it. It looked like the big Cat' was walking on the water and didn't want to get its feet wet.

Of course, the first big rain proved the farmers right. The rice field turned into a brown muddy river draining every foothill for as far as Dan could see. As soon as the rains stopped, Dan hiked out through the mud to see if the road had survived. It was ruined, washed out. There was a big gap where the culverts had been. The force of the high water had swept the culverts downstream and left them bent and useless.

It was a body blow. The people had to slog through the mud, avoiding the offending culverts, trying not to show their sadness and disappointment. They had all worked so hard on the road and were so thrilled when it was done. Now it was just a pile of mud in the middle of the field.

Everyone was upset, but no one complained. It didn't really matter. They had to wait for it to stop raining.

Eventually, the valley drained back to normal and they went back to work, except now they had to wait for a bulldozer again and for the soil to dry up enough to use it.

A bulldozer freed up and Dan got it. This time the Chief didn't complain. There was too much time and effort invested to let the project go now. As soon as the soil was dry enough for the bulldozer to operate without getting stuck they hooked a heavy chain to the culverts and dragged them away from the washout to the side of the field. Ong Wat began making plans for the bridge he wanted all along.

Dan hauled scrap wood to the site. Ong Wat's crew used the wood to set the forms and poured thick concrete abutments about twenty-five feet apart. They traded more scrap wood for more cement and poured a floor of concrete under the bridge to keep it from washing out. When they finally set the steel and poured the span, the bridge looked like a big concrete box that was open on both sides to let the water through.

The bridge was done and the road was open. The villagers came to walk across it, smiling and bowing to one another in the sheer pleasure of witnessing the creation of a long-cherished dream. In the beginning, it had seemed impossible. Now, it seemed like it had always been there. The four hamlets of Hoa An were forever connected.

Chapter Thirty-Six

Dan drove out on to the new road and stopped. A water buffalo grazed along the side of the new road, with a village boy dozing on its broad back. Dan sat in the truck for a moment, then got out and walked to the center of the bridge. A thin trickle of water slipped over the concrete below.

Ong Wat appeared out of the forest and trotted across the new road to greet him. Dan and Ong Wat stood in the middle of the bridge, shaking their heads at the unlikeliness of this feat of faith molded from the mud.

Ong Wat took Dan's hands and spoke to him. A boy translated. "Three days we have party. You come. We eat."

Dan laughed and bowed to Ong Wat. "Thank you. I will be here."

Worked to the last day of its life, a water buffalo had collapsed in the field. The men butchered it where it had fallen, and the women carefully tore the meat into thin, thin strips. These were marinated until the meat was tender and had absorbed the flavors of the special spices of the Nouc Mam fish sauce.

A colorful canopy was erected at the center of the new road. Under it, two large tables were placed end-to-end and covered with fine linen. The men who had worked on the road were seated on one side, facing the women who served the meal of rice, vegetables and water buffalo. The beaming elders stood in a half circle behind the women, smiling. Dan was seated in the middle, with the Vietnamese men to his right and the Americans to his left.

The bright, ancient essence of mysterious delicate spices demanded his attention, and he could see why the European explorers and traders had been so driven to establish trade routes to the 'spices of the orient'. Now they were being set before him in one of the finest meals he had ever eaten.

Offering her most special recipe for the banquet, each woman of the village smiled with pride as she placed it on the table. He carefully took a bite of each and acknowledged his sincere appreciation to the women on the other side of the table.

Each place was set with chopsticks and a big US Marine Corps stainless steel spoon. Looking to his left he watched the Seabees and Marines making a sincere, if awkward, attempt to use their best manners at the table. The Americans had chosen to use the chopsticks and they were starving. It was almost painful to watch them try to drag two or three grains of rice from the plate to their mouths.

Dan turned his head to the right. The Vietnamese men where happily shoveling it in with the big stainless steel spoons.

Chapter Thirty-Seven

One more time Dan squatted with the elders in the shade of the bamboo. They watched a woman walking across the new road. They had dreamed about it for so long and had worked so hard to build it. Now the children could go to school and women could go to market. They were safe and out of the mud. The four hamlets were drawn together, the way they had always dreamed, the way it was supposed to be. The men sat quietly, each in his own thoughts.

Dan thought about how impossible it had seemed just a few months ago. Now, it was like the road and the bridge had always been there. He could hardly imagine the village like it was before.

A little girl crossed on her way to school. A grandfather, shrunken into his white robes, moved slowly across the bridge. He turned, smiled, and raised his cane in salute to the group of men under the bamboo. They bowed and greeted him in turn. He moved carefully, measuring each step as if the road's smooth, broad surface was a strange comfort to his old feet. He turned his head from side to side like he was talking to the ones who had gone on before him, now silently watching over the village from the fields of rice and the forest of bamboo.

"See, we have a new road! I can go visit my new granddaughter! What could be better?"

Dan and the men sipped their tea.

A boy came to interpret for them and they talked together.

"He say road good. Bridge good. He say VC no more."

The elders nodded.

Dan believed them but it still surprised him. The Med-Caps, the new schools, and now the road and the bridge were tying the hamlets together. The people were happy. He could see it on their faces.

The elders talked to him. The boy translated carefully, taking his time to get it right. "They say VC bring guns hide by graveyard."

The boy went on, "He say guns no more. People take guns. Send guns Quang Nam. No more VC. Village chief talk you boss."

Dan pointed to what little brass he had on his hat then in the direction of the base.

"You want to talk to my commanding officer, numba one boss?"

The men all nodded. "Numba one boss."

Dan figured that he had either earned their trust or they had given up on him ever going away. Most importantly, they were offering a relationship that would make it much safer for everyone in the area.

Dan was thrilled. For him, this was Mission Accomplished. This was the reason he was out here in the first place. He knew this so called "war" wasn't over, but that somehow they had *won the peace* for this small part of it. He understood that the village chief was offering every piece of intelligence, everything they knew, and they knew everything.

He was pleased and proud that he had done his part in making this section of Vietnam a little safer for the women and children and the old ones.

It hadn't been easy. He'd lost forty pounds, suffered heat exhaustion three times and barely made it back to the base more than once. His uniform was ragged and his boots were permanently covered with mud.

He left the meeting with the elders, returned to the base and went directly to the Commanding Officer's office. Charlie Davis was now the Battalion clerk. Dan waved at him and walked into the C.O's office to report the good news.

The CO wasn't impressed. He looked at Dan across his desk and said loud and clear. "I ain't talkin' to no gook."

Dan was stunned. The air left his body. How could he have been so wrong? If we weren't there to help protect these people, then what were we doing with all of our guns and our planes and our bombs?

Why had he damn near killed himself working night and day in the village?

The Battalion was not some rogue outfit wreaking havoc under the fog of war. The CO was no better or no worse, than most. Like Dan, he was just doing his duty the way he saw it. Now, Dan could see that for the CO this war had nothing to do with the Vietnamese.

Dan realized he should have known better. I aint' gonna talk to no gook? He should have seen it coming but he had wanted to believe in the mission, his mission, his duty.

He had wanted to believe that if he could work hard enough, risk enough, give enough, maybe he could somehow force it to make sense. They *had* won the peace this day in Hoa An.

Damn it! That counted! It had to. He could not bear to throw it away.

All this flooded through his mind while the CO was talking.

I ain't talking to no gook?

Who in the hell did he think he was? Where in the hell had he come from? Where in the hell did he think he was?

The brutal, horrible unfairness of it overpowered what good judgment Dan had left. It all became a blur and he began to unravel, slowly, then all at once.

Ignoring the CO, he grabbed the door jam and ripped it from the wall. It came off easily. He threw it on the floor, seized hold of the open door and wracked it hard. The top hinge busted and the door fell and hung at a crazy angle. The CO didn't move.

Charlie Davis came into the room, jumped between Dan and the CO, and pushed Dan back and out the door. Dan fell backwards down two steps and landed in the red dirt with Charlie on top of him.

"You're going to the Brig, Dan!" Charlie yelled in a whisper.

On his back in the dirt with Charlie on top of him, Dan calmed down fast. He knew Charlie was right, and he sure didn't want to go to the brig. They got to their feet and dusted themselves off. Dan thanked Charlie for saving his ass. The rage had left him as soon as it had come. Charlie went back up the steps into the CO's office and Dan stood outside waiting.

When he didn't come out after awhile Dan grabbed a box of C-rations and took off to find Ty and Ragatz. For some reason, everything Dan had worked for meant nothing to his command or the country it represented. It was beyond his comprehension. Maybe they thought he was just going out to the village to screw around. It occurred to him that everyone might have been happier if he had.

Ragatz and Ty had set up their camp at the edge of a meadow between Hoa An and Hoa Binh. It was deserted. Dan didn't know what else to do so he moved in and made himself as comfortable as he could.

He was opening the box of C-rats when he looked up and saw Ong Bey with his M1 Garand sitting just inside the bamboo, smiling.

Dan said, "Chao Ong."

Ong Bey nodded at him but didn't say anything.

Dan dug through the C-rations until he found a four pack of unfiltered Lucky Strikes. What the hell did they think this was, Korea?

He held them up for Ong Bey.

The old jungle fighter's face broke into a smile. Dan tossed him the pack of Luckys and Ong Bey tucked it away in his field jacket.

Dan wasn't going to smoke them anyway. He was digging for the Pall Malls. He wondered where Ragatz and Ty were. He looked around their camp and wondered how long they would be gone, and if they were coming back. Ong Bey and his M1 left without a sound.

It was getting dark and Dan was starting to look for a decent place where he wouldn't have to sleep with the rats. There wasn't one.

He heard the marines coming through the brush with just the right combination of care and "it really doesn't matter anyway because we're the Marines" approach to the camp.

Ty came into the clearing first. "Hey, hey, the Seabees have landed."

Ragatz looked at Dan grinning. What else does the 'Bee got in there for us?"

"Just some Pall Malls, some 'fresh' C-rats and some of those mentholated Kools for Ty."

Dan pulled the pack out of his pocket and tossed them to the grateful marine. Ty shook his head, speechless.

They lit up their respective smokes and started to get comfortable.

Dan asked, "You guys been doing anything exciting?"

Ty shook his head.

Ragatz grunted and said, "Yes indeed. We been reportin' in. Had to get some new forms for this 'Vietnamization program'. You heard about it?"

"No, not really."

He told them about Ong Bey being there. "You guys see much of him?"

Ragatz said, "Not much."

Dan asked, "Any of the other PF's?"

Ragatz shook his head, "Not really. It seems like they don't leave Hoa An much."

Dan agreed, "Can't say I blame 'em."

Ragatz lit his Pall Mall and asked,

"What brings you up this way Dan?"

Dan paused, how could things have gone so wrong so fast? He shook his head. "A couple of days ago I met with the elders and they told me the villagers had confiscated the VC's weapons and turned them over to the provincial authorities."

Ragatz looked at him with raised eyebrows. "That's a big deal, man."

"I thought so."

Ty asked, "Where were they cached?"

"On the other side of the graveyard, back there in the bamboo. Where they do their business."

"You mean behind the graveyard where you're having the Med-Caps?"

"Yeah."

Ty raised both arms, fingers in a "V for victory" and laughed, "So, Seabee, you were holding your Med-Caps on top of the VC's weapon cache! No wonder they it gave up!"

It was pretty bizarre, "Mission Accomplished" and AWOL all in one morning. It felt good to laugh. It had been a long time. He didn't know who he was anymore. He realized that AWOL meant no mail, no letter from Lilly. Where the hell was this going?

He wondered what the CO had been thinking. Thank God for Charlie Davis. A few more minutes and he would have been in the Da Nang brig.

Ty pinched out his Kool, saving it for later.

Dan said, "Yeah, you could say I was pretty stoked. I went in right away and told the CO the village chief wanted to meet with him. He just sat there behind his desk looking at me like I was some sort of alien. All he said was, 'I ain't gonna talk to no gook.'"

Ragatz leaned forward with his mouth open. "You gotta be shittin' me."

Dan grunted, "Wish I were. That's what he said."

"That's fucked up man."

"You're tellin' me. I still can't seem to get my mind around it."

"What'd you do?"

Dan shook his head and groaned.

"Aaah, shit – I lost it."

"What do you mean?"

They both looked at him, waiting.

"I started tearing down his hootch."

"The CO's hootch?"

"Yeah."

"What the fuck?" Ty asked, "What did they do to ya?"

"The CO's clerk's a good guy. He saved my ass, tackled me out the door and we landed in the dirt. I cooled down pretty quick and came out here."

Ragatz and Ty stared at him, trying to understand.

Ty shook his head. "You're AWOL mutherfucker."

Ragatz nodded.

"Am I putting you guys in a bad spot?" Dan asked, looking at Ragatz.

"Probably, but who gives a shit? You're the one in the pickle, and you're the one that's gonna have to find a way to take care of it. Other than that, you can hang out with us anytime."

Ty sat nodding and grinning at him. "Welcome to our fine home, Seabee. I'll take first watch. Try to get some sleep if you can."

It had been a long day. Dan rolled up in Ty's extra poncho liner and pulled it over his head to keep the rats off.

He thought about the newspaper Smith had shown him with the map of city after major city going up in the flames of riots about race, inequality, and a war that made no sense to anyone. It still didn't.

He felt that same sort of madness all around him. If we were not there to help these people like we claimed, then it was all just some sort of frantic, insane, American national tantrum suffered by the women and the children and the old papa sans and mama sans who could not defend themselves in a country we never knew and never wanted to know. To people like the CO, they all looked the same. They were all the enemy.

He thought about the packs of American deserters running like a plague through the villages and cities. It seemed like this "war" in Vietnam had nothing to do with the Vietnamese. It was all about us. We knew nothing about them and from what he could tell we didn't want to.

It struck Dan that this "war" in Vietnam was just another battlefield in America's endless civil war with itself. He turned on his side, curled up into a ball and cried in a silent prayer. "Great-grandfather! Father! Mother! What is my duty now? What honor is there when everything I have done has been discarded for nothing?"

He thought of Lilly and how her decency and wisdom had always ridden beside him in the truck. He hadn't felt her there for too long now. How could he hide the shame of his failure from her?

Thinking of her reminded him of her beauty and her smile and the time they had spent together in Hawaii. The truth was, it didn't matter what the Commanding Officer had said or done. He was still the luckiest guy in Vietnam.

He had his forty-five for a pillow. He could see little pinpricks of light from a candle flickering in the homes here and there and hear the murmur of the families talking quietly together. The scent of the fresh food combined with the unique, spicy fragrance of the nouc mam wafted through the forest. Sometimes the candle would appear to flicker and go out, but he knew it was just someone passing in front of the light.

Ragatz shifted his weight in the dark and said, "So you're AWOL, huh Dan?"

"Sorta. Mostly takin' a break, I guess, tryin' to get my head around this crap."

"Thirty days and you're a deserter. You know that, right?"

"Yeah. I just had enough for a while."

Ty said, "You're good with me, Seabee. Thanks for the smokes."

Dan tried to see if there were any stars and twisted around trying to get comfortable.

After a minute he asked, "You guys hear about the G.I. dying with a bag of rats over his head down there south of Hoa An?"

Ragatz rolled toward him, "Yeah, a little scuttlebutt. They didn't tell us much. It's like one of those things they don't wanna discuss. He was dead huh?"

"Yeah."

Ty asked, "Who did it?"

"The villagers said it was deserters."

Ragatz rose up on his elbow waiting for Dan to go on.

"I was down there looking at the school. I guess they thought I should see it. He was tied up in that little clearing just south of the village."

Ty was incredulous. "You found him?"

"What was left of him"

"What'd you do?"

Dan shook his head and looked around their little camp.

"It was messed up man. I didn't know what to do. Got the MP's, but the body was gone when we got back. Other than the MP's, I ain't told nobody but you guys."

"What about your command?"

"They don't want to hear about this shit. Even if they were deserters, who the hell could ever imagine that our guys could do that to another guy? Fuck!"

He gagged on the bile of disgust burning his throat, choked it back down and held it there.

They waited him out then Ty asked quietly.

"Was he black?"

"White."

"What about the guys that did it?"

"Don't know. The villagers didn't say and I didn't ask. Just said they were Numba Ten GI."

Ty's soft voice came out of the darkness. "We got one of those Numba Ten GI's up here too, Dan. Came by the other day, askin' us to help him."

"What'd you do?"

"We didn't know what to do."

Ragatz was on his back looking straight up. Nobody said anything for a long time. Finally Ragatz said, "He's got a wife and a baby out there in the ville' somewhere. He's been out here over two months now. Missed his ticket home."

All Dan could say was, "Shit."

Ty was looking at Dan. "Messed up, huh?"

"What the fuck."

Ragatz said, "We gave him our C-rats. What are you gonna do? They were bringing guys to his hut to fuck his ol' lady. She was scared to death. What about the fucking baby, Dan?"

"Shit, where they livin'?"

"Phouc Toung."

Dan asked, "Why not tell him to come up here and camp out with you guys? Maybe he can straighten things out with his command, offer to re-up or something."

Both marines laughed.

"Sure man, just what'a you think we're doin' out here, running a home for wayward deserters and their dependents?"

Dan had to laugh along with them. It felt good but didn't solve the problem.

After a while he asked, "Why not? She and the baby would be safer up here eating beans and franks with you guys and we can get them to the next Med-Cap, or maybe her family will show up."

Ty waited until it was quiet in the dark. "Who could do such a thing? What kind of person could even imagine something so fucked up?"

No one said anything.

Dan lay awake for most of the night, wondering what in the hell was going on and what could possibly happen next.

Chapter Thirty-Eight

Dan had returned to the base with the Corpsmen after one of the Med-Caps. Nobody asked him where he had been. The letters from Lilly were waiting for him. Hunter looked at him but didn't ask.

Once the bridge was done, Dan and Ong Wat often sat beneath it in the heat of the day. Built like a bunker, it was the safest place for miles around. It was also the coolest. Sometimes, Ong Wat would send one of the boys for beer. They would bring either Tiger beer or Beer 33. He and Ong Wat would drink slowly, watching the water slipping endlessly over the cool concrete.

Today, he was sitting under the bridge by himself. The soft sounds of the village seemed far away. The tiny stream whispered across the rough concrete they had bought with the scrap wood he had hauled to the village. He hadn't hesitated. The wood and tin were too valuable. He'd seized every scrap he could load by hand and hauled it out to the village, making sure it found its way to the right people.

He'd learned the special value of Ong De's "social alchemy." He remembered watching in amazement as his teacher and friend had transformed the trucker's cruel sport into a treasury of scholarships for so many children.

He'd watched Ong De do it again and again, wasting nothing, until it looked like the almost magical result was the only logical outcome. Now they had a bridge and a road and four schools, all paid by scrap on its way to the dump.

Dan leaned back against the coolness of the poured concrete abutment. Wood turned into concrete, both precious, both dear, one becoming the other, doing the job to which they were best suited. Now the water slipped along as the rice grew, the hamlets quietly growing into the newness of being one village.

Dan looked at his hands. The villagers wouldn't even let him get them dirty. He smiled to himself. Maybe they knew something. He imagined his father, bending down, taking a hand full of the soil and turning it between his fingers, holding it to his nose, measuring the harvests to come. He imagined his father squatting with Ong Wat at the edge of the field, talking their farmer talk, the planting, the harvest, the children running barefoot.

He wished his father were here to see this work. Dan missed him and suddenly felt like crying. He wanted to cry and have his Dad poke him in the ribs and joke him out of it, making everything as it should be.

He heard someone sliding down the abutment on the other side. Small rocks rolled down the slope and Ong Wat followed them down. He stepped across the water, smiled at Dan and sat down beside him. Taking Dan's hand he held it on his knee and sat watching the water.

Dan couldn't help it. Unbidden tears slipped out of his eyes and rolled down through the dirt on his face into the corners of his mouth.

Ong Wat patted his hand.

Dan looked at him and said, "You remind me so much of my father."

Ong Wat nodded and patted Dan's hand again.

Dan grinned at him through his tears, "You old farmers sure would hit it off."

Ong Wat looked at Dan and nodded his head. He hummed and pointed across the far ocean to where neither one of them could see. Dan nodded, "Da, father, he farmer like you."

He pointed to Ong Wat then pantomimed digging in the soil.

Ong Wat laughed and said something Dan could not understand. Still holding Dan's hand, he raised both their hands in the air, shook them as in triumph, and slapped them back on his knee. He turned, looked intently into Dan's eyes, smiling and saying something in Vietnamese that Dan didn't have to understand to understand.

Chapter Thirty-Nine

Working with the villagers, they had accomplished more than he had ever imagined. It was good work. Now he was waiting to go home.

He parked the stake-bed on the road near the bridge, opened the door and slid off the seat. He walked to the front of the truck and leaned on the broad front fender. He looked up the rich, green valley toward the foothills. The sights and sounds surrounded him. The scents of the soil, the food, even the bushes on the side of the trail where they picked the leaves for the tea, all mixed together in a sweet, warm fragrance.

Ong Trong, the old mandarin, emerged from the bamboo and with carefully measured steps approached Dan over the new road. This appeared to be an inspection. He stopped in front of Dan and smiled. Dan could tell he was pleased.

He stepped past Dan and with great care stopped at the edge of the bridge. He looked down from the bridge, smiling, stroking his pointy white chin whiskers. He turned, looked at Dan, then folded his arms into his white robes and walked back the way he had come.

A few minutes passed and a young boy ran up and stopped.

"He say road very good. Bridge very good. Good for Hoa An. People happy. He say come tomorrow."

Dan smiled. He went back the next day as requested and parked on the road by the bridge as before.

The elders didn't keep him waiting. They had a job for him, but for some reason couldn't tell him what it was.

They needed certain materials and wanted them dropped at a certain fork in the trail. It was never very much, one or two sacks of cement, or some crushed rock, left at the same fork in the trail.

The cement had to be requisitioned from the Battalion yard where Petty Officer Rodgers was still in charge. Dan didn't have any more Old Crow but Rodgers was going home pretty soon and didn't seem to care one way or the other.

Still, he had to get in his licks, "What do they want it for? You know they're building bunkers with this shit, don't ya?"

Dan shrugged, "I don't know nothin' man. All I know is that they haven't let me down yet."

Rodgers shook his head, "Okay, two sacks of cement."

"How about three?"

"Fine, you know where they are."

"Thanks man, they'll be naming their kids after ya."

Rodgers grinned and shook his head.

"That's Rodgers with a 'D.'"

The fork in the trail. The elders had only asked for one sack of cement but he had seen how carefully they mixed it and how thinly they had spread it to make it go as far as possible. He wanted to make sure they had enough for whatever they were trying to accomplish. He dropped the small loads by the fork in the trail. The next time he came by they were gone.

Chapter Forty

It was late. The base was dark. Dan stepped into the night and closed the door of his little office behind him. The body of a man passed out drunk lay in the shadows of a hootch across the way. He heard the sound of drunk men arguing. He turned and stopped, then stepped back against the wall.

The arguing men came over the hill silhouetted against the night sky. There were three of them, dark shapes, the biggest in the middle. Dan could tell it was Durwood with two of his pals. He didn't move. The guy on the left was waving an M1 Carbine around as he talked. He grabbed Durwood's arm and pointed the carbine at Dan. "Hey, it's the gook lover!"

Durwood didn't see him. "Where?"

"Over there, next to the hootch."

Durwood stopped and grunted, trying to see who it was.

Dan didn't move. He was unarmed, no forty-five, no M16, no knife.

Durwood took a few steps forward and said, "It is the gook lover guys, that White Cong, gook-lovin' bastard."

They spread out. The guy with the Carbine went left and the other guy went right. Durwood took another step toward Dan and stopped. The guy with the Carbine was waving it around like he didn't want it.

For some reason Dan thought about Ong De in the meditation. He brought both hands together in front of him with the fingers pointing up. He felt his center come to him. His vision expanded to where he could see all three of the men at the same time. Everything slowed down. He heard the sounds of other men drinking and yelling somewhere out by the lumberyard.

Durwood lurched toward him and stopped. He looked at Dan's hands. The man on the right broke away from the other two. Circling to come at Dan from the side, he stumbled, and almost fell.

The one with the carbine was backing off still waving the gun, crying, "I'm not gonna shoot nobody, hear me? I'm not gonna!"

Dan made what seemed like eye contact with Durwood through the darkness and held it. Durwood took a couple more steps toward Dan and stopped.

"What you got in your hands gook lover?"

He wanted to say, "Go fuck yourself", but he didn't. He kept his eyes on Durwood, his hands together, fingers pointing upward.

The drunk on the right came at Dan in a rush, stumbled, hit the wall of the hootch and fell. Dan couldn't tell if he was going to get back up or not, but it didn't look like it.

Durwood looked at his pal on the ground, realized he was almost alone and took a step back, muttering his litany of perverted, racist dogma.

Dan held his gaze. Durwood looked away, mumbled something under his breath, stumbled back, lost his balance and sat down hard in the dirt.

Dan stepped over to him, helped him to his feet, and brushed the dirt off his clothes. Durwood was confused. Dan turned him around and sent him on his way.

Chapter Forty-One

"You please come tomorrow."

Dan had gone to the village to say his goodbyes, but the elders had asked him to come back the next day. He was running out of time. He drove to the Bo De School, parked on the highway and walked in. Something was different. He didn't see Ong De or Chaplain Hu. He walked up the steps to the veranda. As always it was cool and quiet.

It had been his classroom, his doorway to Asia. Now it was empty. The English teacher came out and spoke to him. "Ong De? He had to go to Saigon."

"How is he?"

"Not so well. His mother is ill also. Chaplain Hu is also in Saigon. He too has many duties there."

"Please tell them both goodbye for me."

The teacher took Dan's hands in his own and bowed. "I will."

Dan bowed. Overwhelmed by his feelings at leaving this place where he had learned so much, been given so much, he remained bowed, holding the teacher's hands, unable to move.

Finally, he was able to stand erect and say, "Thank you. I must say goodbye now."

He turned, carefully descended the broad steps for the last time then walked slowly across the dirt playground, looking straight ahead. The pain of knowing he would never see his dear friends again drained out on the ground while the bright voices of the children at their lessons came to him through the open windows.

Ong Wat. It was time to go see the old man who was so much like his own father.

He thought of Ba Wi. Like a mother she had told him, "I have son like you. He good boy like you."

Somehow each one of them in their way had shown him the love of a teacher, a mother and a father. Each one of them had found a place in his heart.

He found himself back at the graveyard, back at the road and the bridge.

Now he was leaving the village, the seamstress who gave him safe passage and all the others. He said goodbye to the elders and the children, Ong Bey and the boys who had protected him, the women who worked so hard on the road.

It seemed like parts of him were already gone. Leaving these dear, dear friends, these wise and generous people who had taken him to their heart, was a sadness that lodged in his bones.

Regardless, he was already leaving. Hoa An, his personal Shangri-La, the part of Asia that had taken him in, was already letting him go. Life in the village went on as always. He could feel it already starting to close behind his leaving.

"You please come tomorrow." Like a good son he would do as he was asked.

Mid-morning the next day, the children were in school and the village had settled into the normal routines of day-to-day life. He came in the back way, driving slowly so not to kick up the dust. The seamstress waved and smiled. He wondered how complicated her life had become because of his presence. She had never seemed to mind. He greeted her, parked the truck and got out. He knew they would find him.

It didn't take long before he saw a small parade of elders and friends walking down the road in his direction.

Instead of his white uniform, Ong Trong was wearing something that made him look like the emperor of an ancient Asian dynasty. He was shaded by a multicolored umbrella and he smiled shyly at Dan as the elders approached. They were all there. He saw Ong Wat, Ong Trong, and Ong Thai, and so many others whose names he didn't remember or never knew.

He saw the man in the white shirt who had ridden his bicycle to protect his wife and daughter from the deserter with the hand grenade and "wanted a woman." He was a serious person that day and he was serious now. He bowed stiffly, shook Dan's hand, looked him in the eye, and said, "Cam On."

Dan took his hand in both of his and bowed.

The elders bowed deeply and presented him with a lacquered vase and plate with a village scene. They proudly awarded him a citation from the Provincial Government and a brass medal in the shape of a pagoda that they pinned to his shirt.

As they laughed and bowed and shook his hands, he forgot his sadness about leaving. The elders stepped forward and motioned for him to follow.

They came to the intersection where he had left the supplies they had asked him for. The trail forked to the right into a part of the village where he had never been. They led him along the trail, gently motioning for him to follow.

There was a gate and a carefully landscaped courtyard with a beautifully constructed and ornately decorated shrine canopied by a massive Banyan tree.

He thought of the day he had asked the elders to "meet the priests" and they had patiently tried to tell him they had no priests, and then, when he still failed to understand, they explained that "each father was a priest and each home was a shrine."

Now he was standing in front of an ancient temple on the other side of the world, feeling more at peace and more at home than anywhere he had ever been.

Men from the village were using the materials he had left at the fork in the trail to restore the temple. He bowed, shook their hands and told them goodbye.

He had one more stop. Ong Wat was waiting for him under the bridge with a bottle of Tiger beer.

Dan realized that at the same time the village was telling him goodbye, the world across the sea was already turning to meet him. He was coming home to Lilly who lived in his heart.

He was returning across the sea to his worried mother and father, his brothers and sisters, nephews and nieces, all wondering where he had been and what it was like, and how he had changed. He understood that while they might wonder, they would most likely never ask.

— The End —

Acknowledgments and Gratitude

Connie Ann West for a lifetime of inspiration, support, and understanding, and for writing me a letter every day I was in Vietnam.

Angela West: wise, patient, and understanding daughter.

Michael West: wise, patient, and understanding son.

James West: nephew, editor, and supporter.

Jess West: brother and supporter.

Faye Reimel: sister, reader, and "first fan."

Beth Anderson: portrait, maps, and reader.

Mike Sutherland, Sandy Sutherland, Jerry Friesen, Rebecca Keisler, and Terry Zolezzi: supporters, readers and friends.

Los Osos Writers' Group: Christine Ahern, Anne R. Allen, Laurie Brallier, Stephen Figler, Charlie Perryess, and Sidonie Weidenkeller.

Critique partners: Stephen Figler, Chester Perryess, Eric Schultz.

Carroll Leslie from Volumes of Pleasure Bookshoppe: Advisor, supporter, and friend.

Timber Hawkeye from Hawkeye Publishers: The Good Shepard who did his very best to keep me inside my skin while he wrestled this scaly beast onto the page.